"Traitor," the

A streak of moonli[...]
face, highlighting [...]
the heart-shaped b[...]
Rafael Encizo star[...]
knew the captain.

The officer lashed a fast roundhouse kick to
Encizo's FMK-3 and struck the weapon from his
grasp. He slashed a cross-body karate chop to the
side of the Cuban's skull. The Phoenix fighter
staggered from the blow, and his opponent thrust
stiffened fingers toward Encizo's throat.

"Freeze, you bastard!" Calvin James shouted as
he aimed his M-16 at the man.

The officer slowly raised his arms. For one
second James diverted his attention to watch
Encizo get up. The captain saw his chance and hit
the ground before rolling down a shallow gorge.

"Son of a bitch!" James rasped as he aimed his
rifle at the fleeing officer.

"No!" Encizo cried. He grabbed the rifle barrel
and pushed it toward the sky. "Don't shoot
him!"

"Hey, man," the black warrior snapped as he
shook the gun free of his partner's grasp. "You
crackin' up or something?"

"Don't shoot him, Calvin," Encizo urged. "He's
my brother."

Mack Bolan's
PHOENIX FORCE

#1 Argentine Deadline
#2 Guerilla Games
#3 Atlantic Scramble
#4 Tigers of Justice
#5 The Fury Bombs
#6 White Hell
#7 Dragon's Kill
#8 Aswan Hellbox
#9 Ultimate Terror
#10 Korean Killground
#11 Return to Armageddon
#12 The Black Alchemists
#13 Harvest Hell
#14 Phoenix in Flames
#15 The Viper Factor
#16 No Rules, No Referee
#17 Welcome to the Feast
#18 Night of the Thuggee
#19 Sea of Savages
#20 Tooth and Claw
#21 The Twisted Cross
#22 Time Bomb
#23 Chip Off the Bloc
#24 The Doomsday Syndrome
#25 Down Under Thunder
#26 Hostaged Vatican
#27 Weep, Moscow, Weep
#28 Slow Death
#29 The Nightmare Merchants

PHOENIX FORCE

The Nightmare Merchants

Gar Wilson

A GOLD EAGLE BOOK FROM

WORLDWIDE

TORONTO • NEW YORK • LONDON • PARIS
AMSTERDAM • STOCKHOLM • HAMBURG
ATHENS • MILAN • TOKYO • SYDNEY

First edition May 1987

ISBN 0-373-61329-6

Special thanks and acknowledgment to
William Fieldhouse for his contribution to this work.

Printed in Canada

1

The men waited in the shadows, hiding behind trees and bushes like lions waiting for their prey to move into position. Lieutenant Martinez checked the luminous dial of his wristwatch. One a.m. He frowned. The smugglers were late. They were supposed to have arrived thirty minutes ago. Experience had taught the police lieutenant that drug smugglers were paranoid and extremely cautious. They had to be if they wanted to survive.

"Are you sure that junkie wasn't giving you a load of crap, Lieutenant?" Special Agent Wadsworth muttered as he crouched in the shadows next to the vice cop.

"I don't know why he'd lie," Martinez replied in a weary voice. He had discussed this subject with the Feds before, and it was becoming tiresome. "We told Lopez we'd deal with him, but only if his tip leads to a major bust. Meantime, he's cooling his heels in a cell. If this doesn't pan out, little Lopez will stay in a cage until we can transfer his ass to the state pen. If he's lying to us, that's where he's headed, and he knows it.''

"How much longer are we going to hang around here?" Wadsworth complained, swatting a mosquito on his neck. He cursed under his breath as he stared at the red smear on his hand from the crushed insect. That was his own blood. "Vampire motherfucker."

"Twenty minutes and we close up shop, okay?" Martinez suggested, annoyed by the Fed's lack of patience.

Martinez considered impatience to be a common failing among federal agents in general and those of the Drug Enforcement Administration in particular. Like most local cops, he didn't like dealing with the Feds. Martinez's people were on the streets twenty-four hours a day, gathering information, risking their asses in dangerous undercover assignments. Television made the job look glamorous, but it was really a dirty business where good men mingled with trash who would cut their throats in an instant if they even suspected the guys might be cops.

Instead of lounging around swimming pools with girls in bikinis, Martinez's men hung around seedy dives and slums where junkies bought their dope from street dealers. The worst elements of the drug trade were active in Miami: the Colombian syndicate, which was more ruthless than the Mafia ever thought of being; the *marielitos*, Cuban criminals shipped to the United States in 1980 when Castro decided to empty his prisons and send his convicts to America; the scores of independent groups and the mob-connected big dealers . . . they were all in Miami. These were the adversaries Martinez's people were up against.

The situation was bad, and it was getting worse. Drugs were pouring into the U.S., and Miami was still the favored port of entry. The major crop from south of the border was cocaine, which was slithering into every level of American society.

It astonished Martinez that thousands of people still regarded cocaine as a recreational drug. They claimed it wasn't addictive, that it expanded the consciousness and gave the user more energy and greater awareness. Martinez had one word for those claims: bullshit. He had seen too many girls who turned to prostitution to support their cocaine habit, too many punk thieves who committed armed robbery to buy nose candy, too many blue- and white-collar workers who embezzled money to pay for more white powder. These people committed crimes because they were hooked on cocaine. If that wasn't addiction, what the hell was?

Violence was inevitably associated with the cocaine trade—violence perpetrated by the users and even more by the dealers. The users would lose everything but their craving for coke. They would lose their families, their friends and their jobs. An ounce of cocaine cost more than two thousand dollars—almost seven times more than gold. To pay for their dope, unemployed addicts would bash in people's skulls to rob them of pocket money. They would rob liquor stores and even banks.

These coke thieves were amateurs, frightened, unpredictable and usually paranoid from the effects of cocaine and of the illegal life-style they adopted. A nervous, unstable individual was apt to pull a trigger faster than a calmer, more rational person.

Some users got heavily in debt to loan sharks, who thought nothing of having thugs break their legs—or worse. Female addicts fell in with vicious pimps, who encouraged their drug dependency. The pimps used them like puppets and threatened them, beat them and sometimes killed them if they failed to earn a large enough profit.

But the dealers were the worst of the lot. They turned their customers into slaves. They encouraged their clients to move from snorting coke to free-basing or mainlining or speedballing—mixing cocaine with heroin. Some ruthless dealers would punish the entire family of a customer who failed to pay promptly for the drug. They didn't hesitate to slaughter spouses, children or grandparents as a warning to others.

Recreational drug, my ass, Martinez thought as he squatted behind the bushes with an M-16 assault rifle in his fists. He hated all goddamn dope dealers, but he hated the cocaine peddlers most of all. The fact that the shit was shipped into his city by Hispanics from Colombia, Peru and Bolivia really pissed him off. Martinez was an Hispanic American and proud of it. But the bastards who smuggled dope into the U.S. and the Hispanic hoodlums in America who sold it on the streets were a disgrace to their people.

Of course, it was only a small fragment of the Hispanic community that was associated with the dope business; the drug trade involved lowlife of every race, nation and culture. But the public tended to connect cocaine with Hispanics. That was one more reason why Martinez wanted to stamp out coke dealers and everything they stood for.

Tonight he would make the big bust he had been looking forward to for so long. His men were heavily armed and in position. The DEA was present because it fought the same battle on the federal level. Of course, the Feds got most of their intel from local police departments, and they had to rely on men like Martinez to set up operations like this one. Martinez's people had done all the legwork, learned all the details and taken all the risks until they had finally learned the destination of the shipment of Colombian coke that was due to arrive tonight in the belly of a twin-engine Beech aircraft.

So Special Agent Wadsworth and his boys would participate in the bust. Fine. Martinez figured they couldn't screw up the investigation, because it was finished. All that remained was for the damn dealers to arrive so they could grab the bastards. The plane was supposed to be carrying almost one hundred kilos of cocaine. One hundred kilos of misery and human destruction that would never reach the streets of Miami . . .

"Hey, you hear that?" Detective Lockwood, one of Martinez's vice cops whispered. "Sounds like the guests of honor have finally arrived."

The hum of engines grew louder, and a pair of lights appeared in the night sky. The plane was slowly approaching the small dirt runway. The headlights of two vehicles cast bright beams of light along a pathway near the landing area. The smugglers were arriving, and their buyers were ready for them. Martinez's blood rushed with excitement.

"This is it, gentlemen," he announced tensely. "Everybody wait for my signal before you move. We don't want anybody to get suspicious."

"Congratulations, Lieutenant," Wadsworth commented as he unsheathed his .38 snub-nosed revolver, a weapon that was virtually useless at one hundred yards.

"Save it until we've finished our job," Martinez barked.

The plane was descending to the runway. The cops and DEA agents hidden beyond the tree line could see the shape of the aircraft. The extended wings of the Beech resembled twin surfboards jutting from the oblong body. The landing gear drew closer to the ground. The headlights of the two land vehicles turned toward the trees where the law-enforcement officers were hidden.

"Don't worry," Martinez assured his men. "They can't see us. They're just being careful."

Suddenly the plane angled upward, rising above the runway without landing. It climbed higher and cruised directly over the trees where the cops and agents were concealed. A barrel-shaped object dropped from the plane as it flew overhead.

"What the f—" Detective Lockwood began as the object plunged to earth. His words were lost in the roar of a mighty explosion.

The explosion killed at least four cops instantly. A wave of flaming chemicals splashed across the forest, burning both vegetation and human flesh. Men screamed, and some staggered from the unholy blaze shrouded in angry yellow flame.

Martinez and Wadsworth managed to dash from the inferno unscathed. Lockwood followed. He howled in agony, his back covered with fire that danced from his buttocks to the hair at the back of his skull. The three men ran right into the brightly lit paths laid down by the headlights of the two vehicles.

The metallic chatter of an automatic weapon erupted. Machine gun bullets crashed into the torsos of Martinez, Wadsworth and Lockwood. Their bodies twitched and hopped from the impact until the stream of high-velocity slugs shifted away to spray the tree line. The machine gun continued to snarl until the gunners had exhausted one third of an 800-round ammo belt through the breech of the weapon.

"*¡Detenerse, compañeros!*" the leader of the murderous team at the vehicles instructed. "*¡Está bien asada el policía!*"

The others ceased fire and laughed at their team leader's joke that the cops had been well roasted, as if they were meat cooking for a barbecue.

"*¡Muy bien!*" the boss praised his men as he stuck a long, twisted cheroot in his mouth. He lit the cigar and added in a gruff tone, "*¡Anda! ¡Date prisa! ¿Comprende?*"

Indeed they all understood the need to hurry from the site. They hastily loaded the machine gun into the back of a slate-gray minivan and climbed into the vehicles. The leader slid into the back seat of an old Chevy sedan. His cheroot jutted from beneath a bushy black mustache as he smiled at the driver.

"*¿Muy divertido?*" he asked the squat bearded man behind the steering wheel.

"*Sí, Señor Benitez.*" The driver confirmed that he, too, had enjoyed their work that night.

Carlos Benitez took the cigar from his mouth and blew a smoke ring out the window as the car followed the van up the path. He gazed back at the burning forest and inhaled the sweet stench of charred flesh. Gringo cops burning. It smelled lovely to Benitez—like the aroma of a good steak, or perfume on the neck of a beautiful woman.

They drove out of the forest and headed for the highway. Benitez started to sing "O Amante de la Cocaina." The other men in the car joined in the song.

2

The men of Phoenix Force sat at the conference table in the war room of Stony Man headquarters, grimly watching the wide-screen television set. They viewed a videotape of charred corpses being hauled from a pile of ashes and burned tree trunks. The police and paramedics who carried the grisly remains on stretchers looked nauseated. One young police officer vomited onto the blackened grass.

"Fourteen bodies," Hal Brognola announced as he switched off the VCR and turned to face Phoenix Force. "Nine Miami police officers and five federal agents from the DEA. Most burned to death. The others were killed by a light machine gun—7.62 mm bullets. Full-ball military ammunition, probably fired from an M-60 machine gun. Judging from the shell casings and the damage caused by the gunshots, the killers fired more than two hundred rounds at the cops."

Brognola stuck an unlit cigar in his mouth and chewed the butt angrily. He had been a federal agent for nearly twenty years. He took the murder of law-enforcement personnel very hard.

Hal Brognola had risen to the top of his profession. He had reached a level of authority that was probably greater than that of the director of the CIA or FBI. Brognola was the chief of operations of Stony Man, a top-secret organization set up to take direct action against international terrorism, organized crime and threats to the well-being of the United States and the nations of the free world.

Stony Man had originally been based upon the unique abilities and experience of the one-man army known as the Executioner. Mack Bolan had proved his extraordinary skill and resourcefulness during his single-handed war against the Mafia. Incredibly Bolan had not only survived, he had crushed many of the czars of organized crime.

The President had offered Bolan a new war against an even more ruthless and potentially far more dangerous adversary—the modern Vandals known as terrorists. Bolan had accepted the challenge. Officially Mack Bolan had died in his final battle against the mob. But the Executioner lived on as Colonel John Macklin Phoenix.

Colonel Phoenix and Hal Brognola had built Stony Man operations, forming two teams of highly trained warriors to combat the growing wave of terrorism. Able Team was composed of three of Bolan's comrades-in-arms from the Mafia wars. The five members of the second unit had been personally selected by the Executioner. With different backgrounds and varied skills, they were experts in antiterrorism, covert combat *and* kicking ass. They were Phoenix Force—a new kind of Foreign Legion for a new kind of war.

A lot had changed since then. Colonel John Phoenix had been framed by the KGB and had become a renegade once more. Keio Ohara, the tall Japanese electronics wizard and martial arts expert among the original five men of Phoenix Force, had been killed in battle. Perhaps if the world had suddenly become a gentler, safer place, the President would have ordered Brognola to disband the outfit. But sinister new threats to the free world had forced the President to turn to Stony Man for help.

Terrorism was only one of many dragons the men of Phoenix Force had to slay. Their battlefields were all over the world; their success rate was one hundred percent. Now Brognola had a new assignment for the five battle-hardened warriors. He leaned against the table as he addressed Phoenix Force.

"The fourteen law-enforcement officers were at a stakeout about thirty miles north of Miami. They were waiting to bust a planeload of cocaine that was supposed to land at a small airstrip at a clearing in the forest. Apparently the smugglers knew the cops were there. The plane flew over the stakeout position and dropped a firebomb on them, and then the bastards with the chopper finished the job."

"Strange behavior," Rafael Encizo remarked, drumming his fingers on the tabletop. "If they knew about the stakeout, they could simply have made the drop somewhere else. Instead, they went out of their way to kill those guys."

As a youth in Cuba, Encizo had fought the Communists after Castro's soldiers had brutally murdered his father, mother and older brother. His younger brother and two sisters had been taken to a "reeducation center" to learn the truth according to St. Marx. The Encizo family had been victims of the revolutionary zeal that had swept through Cuba in 1959. Young Rafael had joined a small band of counterrevolutionaries who had fought bravely but hopelessly against the Communist police state. Eventually, he had escaped to the United States.

On April 17, 1961, Rafael Encizo returned to Cuba in the Bay of Pigs invasion. The attempt to overthrow Castro was doomed before the freedom fighters reached the beach. Many were killed.

Encizo was sent to Castro's notorious political prison, El Principe. He was starved, beaten and tortured, but he never broke. His jailers, however, thought he was beginning to embrace the doctrines of communism, and got careless. Encizo broke a storm trooper's neck and escaped from Cuba again.

This time he became a naturalized U.S. citizen, working as a diving instructor, a professional bodyguard, a treasure hunter and a maritime insurance investigator. Occasionally he accepted a mission into

Central and South America on behalf of law-enforcement agencies but, wary after the Bay of Pigs, he didn't trust the intel networks.

However, the invitation to join Phoenix Force was different. Phoenix Force was an elite group of experts who took direct action largely on their own. No one promised air support or field artillery. The honesty about the risk involved was what most impressed Encizo. The offer had been too intriguing to refuse.

"Seems to me this isn't the first time DEA agents and vice cops have been killed at a stakeout," Gary Manning commented. "It's a dangerous profession."

Manning was a big Canadian, built like a professional football player. He was also a world-class demolitions and explosives expert and a superb rifle marksman who had worked with the Fifth Special Forces in Vietnam and had conducted several missions behind enemy lines. Manning was one of the few Canadian citizens to be awarded the Silver Star during the Vietnam conflict.

After Vietnam he was recruited to serve in the newly formed antiterrorist branch of the Royal Canadian Mounted Police. For training in combating urban terrorism, Manning was sent to West Germany, where he worked with the elite GSG-9 antiterrorist squad in the 1970s.

By the time Phoenix Force was formed, Manning was back in Canada and working with North American International. The invitation to join the unique band of warriors had appealed to his adventurous spirit and he had readily accepted.

Brognola nodded at Manning. "Drug-enforcement agents and cops have been killed in the line of duty before," he confirmed. "But this time they were set up to be slaughtered. The bastards weren't trying to make a delivery. They planned to murder those men."

"Any idea who *they* might be?" David McCarter inquired, taking a pack of Player's cigarettes from the inside pocket of his rumpled sport jacket.

The fox-faced Briton wasn't a snappy dresser, but he never claimed to be. He had devoted his life to developing his skills as a fighting man.

He had certainly succeeded. McCarter was a former officer in the Special Air Service, who had seen action in Oman and Northern Ireland. He was one of the SAS commandos who had conducted the stunning raid on the Iranian embassy in London in 1980 and had also participated in covert "police action" in Hong Kong.

A superb pilot, an Olympic-level pistol marksman and an expert in unconventional warfare, McCarter had been an obvious choice for Phoenix Force. Although an unashamed thrill junkie, he also possessed the principles and dedication for the job.

"There isn't much doubt who's responsible for the slaughter in Florida two nights ago," Brognola answered. "It's the drug runners. Organized drug runners. Either Mafia or the Colombian syndicate...or a combination of the two."

"Or MERGE," Manning said grimly.

He referred to a little-known but extremely powerful criminal network. After Mack Bolan's war against the Mafia, remnants of the mob had joined forces with the Corsican syndicate, the increasingly powerful Colombian syndicate and the so-called Mexican Mafia.

The latter, mainly involved in dope smuggling and dealing, loan-shark operations and protection rackets, had greatly increased its influence when it had become part of MERGE. The power of the Colombian syndicate, too, had grown, along with the steady increase in supply and demand for cocaine. Membership wasn't limited to Colombians but included citizens of many South and Central American countries, and from the United States as well. With the connections and manpower made available through the MERGE alliance, the already fearsome crime organizations became increasingly dangerous.

"Murdering DEA agents and vice cops sounds like MERGE," Encizo commented, "although it could be just the Colombians. Just last year, the syndicate offered a bounty for U.S. narcotics agents operating in Colombia and Bolivia—thirty thousand dollars for each Fed their hit men could deliver...dead or alive."

"God knows they can afford to pay top dollar for assassins," Brognola said, jabbing a finger at a file folder on his desk. "I've got some recent reports here on the cocaine business. The white powder rakes in close to one hundred billion dollars a year. I see a lot of scary shit come into this office, but I seldom see anything scarier than that. That kind of money can buy and sell governments, not just individual lives."

"Narcotics has always been an ugly business," Yakov Katzenelenbogen remarked, tapping an onyx ashtray with the steel hooks attached to the stump of his right arm. "But it usually doesn't concern Phoenix Force. I take it the President wants us to get involved because the security of the DEA has obviously been burned?"

"As usual," Brognola replied, "you're right, Katz."

"It hardly required the IQ of an Einstein to figure it out," Katz said modestly.

Yakov Katzenelenbogen was the unit commander of Phoenix Force. Middle-aged with a slight paunch, a man of culture and civility, Katz didn't fit the stereotype of a fighting man or espionage agent. Yet he had nearly forty years of experience as both.

In the 1940s, when most of his family were victims of the Holocaust, the young Katz had fought the Nazis with fiery determination. His fluency in languages had been useful to the French Resistance and later to the American OSS.

At the end of World War II, Katz emigrated to Palestine and joined in the Israeli struggle for independence. It was during the Six-Day War that he lost his only son and his right forearm.

The amputation didn't discourage Katz from hunting down Nazi war criminals, leading raids on terrorist bases and outsmarting KGB agents as a member of

Mossad, Israel's primary intelligence network. He was so valuable that the Israeli government loaned him to the CIA, the British SIS, the French Sûreté and the West German BND. The zenith of his career was his appointment as unit commander of Phoenix Force.

Katz had a question for Brognola. "Have there been any similar incidents anywhere else recently?" he asked.

"Unfortunately, yes," Brognola replied. "The attack in Florida the other day isn't an isolated incident. A similar slaughter took place near the Texas border four days ago, and another in Baja California. And we have reports of the same thing in Colombia, Bolivia and possibly Peru. Cops and government agents stake out an arca where a drug deal is supposed to go down, and they wind up in an ambush."

"So the dudes assigned to stop the coke traffic have become targets," Calvin James commented, shaking his head. "I can see why the President is upset. If this continues, the cops and the Feds will be too busy covering their asses to stop that shit from getting into the country."

James was the most recent addition to Phoenix Force, a tall, athletic black man from the south side of Chicago. A tough childhood had proved to be the foundation of a very tough man.

At age seventeen, Calvin James became a hospital corpsman in Vietnam with the Sea, Air and Land unit, a naval commando team. SEALs were trained in underwater combat and demolitions, parachute jumping, small arms, hand-to-hand combat—all the skills of an elite warrior class. In Southeast Asia, James found that the law of the jungle was even deadlier than in the mean streets of his youth.

After Vietnam, James at first studied medicine and chemistry in California on the GI bill, but the violent deaths of his mother and his sister led him to change course. He became a police officer in San Francisco and soon joined the Special Weapons and Tactics squad. Phoenix Force had drafted James for a mission against the Black Alchemist terrorists, and he had remained with the Force ever since.

"That's right, Calvin." Brognola nodded, chewing the cigar butt angrily. "The President wants these butchers taken care of. So do I. You guys are experts. Frankly, it's kind of a screwed-up assignment, because I don't even know where you should start."

"The first thing we have to do is find the moles in the DEA and maybe some of the corrupt cops in vice," Katz announced. "If we can find them, they'll lead us to who pulls their strings and then to whoever is behind them."

"You make it sound easy, Katz," the Fed replied.

"If it was easy, we wouldn't be given the mission," Katz said with a smile. "What we need is somebody reliable in DEA. Somebody who can't be corrupted by the lure of millions in payoff money. And don't kid yourself, Hal. Such men are rare...even among law-enforcement personnel."

"There are still men who can't be bought at any price," Brognola said stiffly.

"Of course there are," the Israeli colonel agreed. "We have a roomful of them right here. But you can't be blinded by prejudice in favor of law-enforcement officers, especially federal officers. Sad fact is, few are above corruption."

"I know a guy in DEA we can trust," Brognola stated. "Harold Krebs. I've known the man for more than ten years. He's a personal friend. I'd trust him with my life."

"How about with ours?" James asked dryly.

"If Hal vouches for the guy," Encizo declared, "I figure we can trust him."

"What's Krebs's status with the DEA?" Manning inquired.

"Assistant deputy director," the Fed replied. "About fourth from the top."

"Good," Katz said. "We'll need somebody with access to personnel records, details about past operations, investigations into the previous incidents— someone who can supply data about drug busts planned for the near future."

"Sounds like you're already formulating a strategy," Brognola commented, impressed by how quickly Phoenix Force had gotten a grip on the situation.

"Bit too early to do that," Katz confessed. "We can't really decide how to handle the situation until we learn more about it. Frankly, we can't promise we'll be able to do anything."

"Oh," Brognola said in a subdued voice.

"Sorry, Hal," Encizo told him, "but Yakov is right. I've been attached to DEA and border patrol a few times in the past. Drug smugglers are the very worst to deal with. There are thirty-seven federal organizations trying to keep cocaine out of the country and to stop the harvesting of the crops in South America. Hundreds of state and local police departments have been part of the effort, too. It's unrealistic to expect us to do any better than they have."

"Well," McCarter began with a wolfish grin, "we're a bit more experienced playing hardball with bastards who don't follow the rules. We don't pay that much attention to the rule book ourselves."

"I don't care if you have to throw it out for this mission," Brognola told them. "Do whatever you have to do to get results. I'll make that real clear. Find out who's responsible for this, apprehend them if you can, but if there's no other way—kill the bastards."

"We're not assassins, Hal," Manning reminded him.

"I didn't say you should assassinate anyone," the Fed assured him. "The men you're looking for are murderers and dealers in a substance that ruins people's lives and causes them to commit all sorts of crimes to support their habit. The dope peddlers are responsible. So punish the guilty."

"Punish?" Encizo raised an eyebrow.

"Capital punishment," Brognola replied simply.

3

The monkey squatted on the floor of its cage and slapped a paw against one of the two levers mounted on the wall of the pen. The little primate seemed anxious. Its shoulders quivered and its teeth chattered. Its bright green eyes darted from side to side as it frantically slapped the lever.

"This little fella is a cocaine addict," Harold Krebs explained, leading the members of Phoenix Force through an experimental laboratory of the Allison Research Clinic in Washington, D.C. "If he hits the right-hand lever, he gets food. The lever on the left is for cocaine. Notice which one he's hitting. Left to his own devices, this monkey will starve to death. Given a choice between coke and food, he'll pick cocaine every time."

"So much for the popular belief that cocaine isn't physically addictive," Rafael Encizo remarked with a sigh, watching the monkey desperately striking the lever.

"Monkeys aren't too big on psychological addictions," Krebs said with a nod. "Cocaine is the only drug they react this dramatically to. You can give them alcohol, hashish oil, marijuana, even heroin. Oh, you'll get a monkey that's an addict, but he won't starve himself for any drug except cocaine.''

"Guess you might say this monkey's got a person on his back," Calvin James muttered but he wasn't smiling at his attempt at a joke. He felt sorry for the poor little animal. It looked so panicked, so desperate for a fix. James had seen that expression on human faces more often than he cared to think about.

"Cocaine is the only drug monkeys will keep taking until it kills them," Krebs continued. "The poor little bastards keep taking it until they go into convulsions, and their hearts finally give out."

Gary Manning looked angry. "I don't want to sound like a bleeding heart," he said, his voice revealing his tension, "but is this sort of thing necessary? Animal abuse rubs me the wrong way, Krebs."

"You'd rather they did experiments on people?" Krebs replied with a shrug. Though close to sixty, he was a big man with broad shoulders and a barrel chest, and he wasn't easily intimidated.

"You already know what cocaine does to monkeys," Manning insisted. "Why continue these experiments?"

"Krebs isn't responsible for the research done at this institution," Yakov Katzenelenbogen reminded the Canadian.

"That's true," Krebs stated. "But I'll answer the question anyway. Monkeys are still being given dope in an effort to try to find better ways of treating cocaine addiction in people. The researchers here hope to come up with something like methadone or naltrexone, drugs that are currently used to treat heroin addicts.''

"I understand there's a problem with methadone because it can be addictive, too," Encizo commented. "I've never heard of the other drug before."

"You're right about methadone being addictive," the DEA man confirmed. "But it takes a lot longer to get hooked on it than on heroin. The idea is to ease the addict out of dependency and then get him to abstain altogether. Naltrexone isn't addictive, at least not physically, but it can't be used on a person with liver damage. That means most hard-core addicts can't use it. Liver damage is common with coke addicts."

"I hope you're referring to cocaine and not Coca-Cola," David McCarter commented. The Briton had developed a fondness for the soft drink during his years in Oman, Vietnam and Hong Kong.

"Oh, yeah," Krebs assured him. "But you know, Coca-Cola did actually contain cocaine when it first came on the market."

"Christ!" McCarter looked shocked. "You're kidding?"

"Nope," the DEA agent said with a shake of his head. "That's where it got its name. Coca-Cola originally contained an ingredient from the leaves of the coca plant. Don't worry though. Coke, the soft drink, doesn't contain cocaine anymore. The company dropped cocaine from the formula a long time ago when people first learned how dangerous the drug could be. Too bad they have to learn all over again.''

"What do you mean?" James inquired as Krebs led them from the lab. They walked toward an elevator, down a hospital-clean corridor with stark white walls and smooth tile floors.

"I mean, cocaine isn't new," Krebs answered. "Hell, Indians in South America have been chewing coca leaves for centuries. Chewing a wad of leaves all day is a mild stimulant, like a cup of coffee. But leave it to the white man to screw around with something that's relatively harmless and turn it into something that'll cause widespread misery. Around 1855 some smartass found a way to isolate cocaine and made the shit into a drug."

"It's been around that long?" Manning raised his eyebrows with surprise.

"Sure," Krebs answered, waving the others into the elevator ahead of him. "Used to be perfectly legal less than a hundred years ago. Hospitals used it as an anesthetic. In the 1880s dozens of products containing cocaine were sold to the public. Medicines for toothache, for indigestion and nerves. There was even a popular French wine that contained cocaine."

"Mariani coca wine," Katz commented.

"That's right." The DEA man raised an eyebrow. "How'd you know about it?"

"My father mentioned it," Katz answered. "He said it was very popular for a long time before people realized cocaine might be more than a harmless stimulant.''

"Mariani coca wine was sold for about twenty-three years," Krebs stated. "Thomas Edison drank it. So did Jules Verne, and even Pope Leo XIII endorsed it. Frederic Bartholdi, the guy who designed the Statue of Liberty, once received a bottle as a gift. He said if he had started drinking it earlier, the statue would have been several meters higher.''

"He might have been a few meters higher himself," McCarter commented with a shrug.

The elevator doors opened, and Krebs escorted Phoenix Force along another antiseptic-white corridor.

"I recall that Sigmund Freud experimented with cocaine," Katz stated. "He even prescribed it for patients, didn't he?"

"That's right," Krebs confirmed. "But that was before it was known that coke was habit-forming. It took an increase in cocaine-related crime to show that the drug was downright dangerous. Statistics claim sixty percent of all violent crime in the early twentieth century was connected with cocaine addiction. And now we're going through the same rotten mess all over again.''

"This is all very interesting, Mr. Krebs..." Manning began, a trace of a sigh in his voice.

"Just call me Harry, okay?" Krebs urged. "I thought Hal would have told you guys I don't like formalities. Now, you're asking yourselves why I insisted you fellas meet me here at the clinic, right?''

"We did wonder," Katz admitted.

"It's because I want to make sure you guys know how bad the problem really is," Krebs insisted. "It's estimated that more than twenty million Americans have tried cocaine. Three out of four wind up abusing it. At least one out of four gets addicted. And the problem keeps getting worse. Every day approximately five thousand Americans try coke for the first time. Those are frightening statistics."

Krebs stopped in front of a closed office door, rapped on it, then opened it. The small room contained two dark leather armchairs, an angular couch and a plain metal desk. A slender bearded man sat behind the desk. On the wall nearest him were three framed diplomas and two plaques. He smiled as he got to his feet.

"These are the visitors I told you about, Doc," Krebs announced. He turned to Phoenix Force. "This is Dr. Michael Garrison, the clinic doctor."

"Pleased to meet you," Garrison said. He gestured toward the couch and chairs. "Please sit down. I think Harry wants me to tell you about some of my patients. You want lots of details or an edited version?"

"I'm afraid we don't have much time, Doctor," Katz replied.

Garrison nodded. "Well, we get all sorts in here. Mostly middle-class folks. The belief that cocaine is only used by the rich is as false as most politicians' campaign promises. Sure, you hear about the movie stars and rock singers who get arrested, the comedians and senators' kids who die from overdoses. But the fact is, it's mostly ordinary people who get hooked on cocaine. Students, construction workers, teachers, housewives, auto mechanics, you name it. Cokers are in every profession. Some of the worst cases are in my profession. Doctors have easy access to drugs. They think they can handle it. Even when they realize they have a problem, they're the least likely to seek help.''

"You mean medical doctors?" Manning inquired.

"Cardiologists, plastic surgeons, psychiatrists." Garrison shrugged. "All sorts. They go to some party where coke is available and decide to give it a try. Cocaine has a special appeal to the user. It produces a paradoxical effect that even most medical personnel aren't prepared to handle."

"They get high, right?" McCarter said. It seemed obvious to the Briton.

"It's more than that," Garrison explained. "The euphoria speeds up the heart, elevates blood pressure, increases the flow of adrenaline. Now that's both exciting and frightening, but the paradox is that the brain sends a message that everything is just fine. The person has a feeling of exhilaration, and an illusion of control. He believes he's thinking more clearly, acting with greater energy. Many cocaine users think it has an aphrodisiac affect. Freud believed that, too. A lot of my patients say they felt invincible the first time they used cocaine. That's a real rush. They want to do it again.''

"And again and again and again," Encizo commented.

"You got it," the doctor confirmed. "Cocaine is a self-stimulating drug. The more you use, the more you want . . . and the more you have to use to get the desired effect. However, most addictive drugs are like that. How is cocaine different? An alcoholic usually drinks for years before his body builds up a tolerance and he needs to down a fifth of booze to get a buzz. But the effects of regular coke use show up a lot sooner. And the physical and psychological effects are very destructive. Skin abscesses, liver damage, dead brain cells. The sinuses go through hell. I've got patients who destroyed their nasal membranes and had to have them replaced surgically with Teflon fibres. Even what appears to be a relatively mild symptom, lack of appetite, leads to bone disease, anemia, severe malnutrition.''

"Yeah," Krebs agreed. "But the mental effects are even worse.''

"That's right," Garrison said. "It's not surprising that the initial sense of euphoria doesn't last. The body is going through hell. Along with the circulatory and nervous system problems, the liver is overloaded. Sometimes the user experiences hallucinations. It's hard to say whether cocaine itself actually causes hallucinations, or whether they're caused by the lack of sleep resulting from cocaine use, but they happen, anyway. Individuals get restless, irritable, hostile, paranoid, sometimes violent.''

"And they usually try to treat the psychological symptoms by using more cocaine, which just makes them worse," Krebs added.

"Don't they sometimes try to cut the effect by using some kind of sedative?" Encizo asked. "Alcohol or maybe Quaaludes?"

"Yes, indeed," Garrison agreed. "Many people currently being treated for cocaine abuse were originally alcoholics. They drank so much to counteract the cocaine, they wound up with two drug problems instead of one."

"Coke freaks will do anything to get their fix," Krebs commented. "In that respect at least, a coke addict isn't any different from a heroin addict."

"Cocaine is just as bad as heroin," Garrison stated firmly. "I'm convinced of that. If anything, it's worse, because coke is accepted in many circles where heroin isn't. Of course, a lot of crime can be connected to cocaine. Take the bank run in Ohio in March of 1985 A number of loan outfits folded. It was a multimillion-dollar scandal that turned out to be connected to a Florida-based corporation with top personnel who were helping themselves to tons of cash. A lot of that money was being spent on cocaine."

"Cocaine addicts embezzle money from their businesses, sell the mortgages on their houses...there was even one case where a woman sold her baby to an il legal adoption agency to get money for coke,'' Krebs declared. "Not to mention prostitution and armed robbery for the same reason."

The men of Phoenix Force looked at one another. Krebs and Garrison hadn't really told them anything about the connection between cocaine and crime that they didn't already know. The recital of the drug's devastating personal and social consequences was overwhelming, but not of much help to them in accomplishing their mission.

"Well, we appreciate the rundown on cocaine—" Manning began wearily.

Krebs interrupted. "Wait a minute, pal. We're not finished yet. You guys still have a few more things to learn about coke. I assume none of you have ever used snow?"

"Never even drank Inca herb tea," James answered.

"You'll need to be able to recognize cocaine," the DEA agent stated. "We've got a little chemical kit that will test the purity of coke—you can't tell purity by just tasting it."

"I've used those kits before," Encizo said with a shrug. "I'll show the others. Anything else we need to know?"

"Just a rundown on recent routes used by smugglers, and some things I'll tell you when we're done." Krebs turned to the doctor. "You understand?"

"I don't want to understand," Garrison assured him, raising his hands as if to fend off an invisible attack. "Your job is to keep coke out of the country and off the street. My job is to help the people who get hooked on the stuff that slips past you. God knows, there's tons of it out there."

"How effective is the treatment for cocaine addiction?" Katz inquired, genuinely curious.

"About the same as for any other kind of drug abuse," Garrison answered. "We've been dealing with alcoholics for decades, and the best we can say is about thirty-five percent will get off the bottle and stay off. The others go right back to drinking until they wind up in a psychiatric hospital, a prison or a cemetery. It's too early to say how many cocaine addicts stay cured, but we figure maybe twenty percent. The users who just snort it have a better chance than those who free-base or shoot it up. Of course, the real problem isn't cocaine. It's the fact that there's a demand for the drug to begin with."

"You mean if people weren't willing to pay for cocaine there wouldn't be any addiction," Encizo said, looking thoughtful. "Or any traffic in the stuff."

"Exactly," Garrison said with a nod. "It's the demand for mind-altering substances that's at the root of addiction. Drug abuse has been a major problem for decades, and it will continue to be a major problem until people no longer feel the need to screw up their heads with booze, pills, powders and intoxicating weeds."

"You think that's likely to happen?" James asked.

"Hell, no," Garrison said with a sigh.

4

The fortress stood in the Amazon jungle at the Colombia-Peru border. It was built of stone and mortar, with heavy shatter-resistant glass windows. Sentries armed with automatic weapons and trained attack dogs patrolled the grounds. Two machine guns were mounted within semicircles of sandbags.

Although the emphasis on security detracted from the elegance of the estate, it still possessed remarkable beauty. Baroque-style statues stood at the corners of a swimming pool eight meters long and five meters wide. The house itself featured gargoyles and cherubim carved into the walls and extending from the window ledges.

Inside the house was more evidence of the owner's love of art. Original oil paintings, including two genuine Picassos, hung on the walls. Priceless jade figures from Thailand and Japan were displayed in glass cases, and several Louis Quatorze chairs and couches figured in the furniture.

One display case featured ancient Indian art. Mayan figures of stone and pre-Columbian pottery lined one shelf. An Aztec calendar and a fuchsine mask adorned with shells and cinnabar were on another shelf. On the third shelf were gold and silver jewelry and statuettes. Earrings with tiny gold faces, reliefs of Tupac Yupangui and tiny figures of panpipe players and warriors armed with spears and clubs were included in the rare and valuable collection.

Although he was of Spanish descent, El Tiburón was very proud of his ancient Indian relics. He enjoyed telling visitors about the legend of the Incan curse, which claimed the coca leaf would make the Indians strong but would eventually destroy the white men.

For several years El Tiburón, "the Shark," had led the "Bolivian Mafia" known as El Dorado, which had long been closely associated with the Colombian syndicate. MERGE had chosen him to command their new counterattack force because the Shark had earned a reputation for success in such matters in the past.

In Bolivia and Peru, he had led counteractions against the million-dollar American programs to destroy coca crops and to track down members of the coke trade. His hired assassins had kidnapped and murdered nineteen members of an American-sponsored unit trying to eradicate coca bushes near the Peruvian Andes. Four of the victims had been tortured before they were killed.

El Tiburón had also arranged the murder of a prominent Catholic priest in La Paz. He had personally supervised the torture and murder of seven police informers in Peru, cutting the throats of all seven himself.

El Tiburón was no coward. He had once been attacked by three hoodlums from a rival drug gang in Lima. He had drawn a compact Italian-made derringer and fired two .38 caliber slugs into the chest of the nearest opponent. The other two had closed in to cut him to ribbons, but El Tiburón had drawn his own dagger. Adept with a knife, he had quickly dispatched one opponent and wounded the other. Clutching his slashed wrist, the injured hood had cursed and fumbled in his belt for a pistol. El Tiburón had lunged as the thug's gun had snarled. A 9 mm slug had slammed into El Tiburón's side, but only cracked a rib. The Bolivian drug czar had buried his blade in the gunman's throat and watched him die.

The leaders of the Colombian syndicate and MERGE respected El Tiburón. He was an excellent planner and coordinator, bold yet cunning, and careful. And he specialized in murder.

El Tiburón sat behind his massive white oak desk. The forty-four-year-old Bolivian gangster was a physical fitness fanatic who was careful with his diet and swam ten laps every morning. Ironically the cocaine king didn't smoke or drink, let alone indulge in his deadly product.

His face was handsome, with a strong jaw, bow-shaped mouth and slightly crooked nose. A slight scar from an old knife wound only enhanced his appearance, and a few gray streaks lent distinction to his curly black hair.

Attracting women was no problem for El Tiburón, but he was fastidious about females. He had four mistresses, in Panama City, in Lima, in Bogotá and in Miami. His wife, known as Señora Veaga, and their children lived in La Paz. She had only a vague idea what her husband, whom she called Pedro, did for a living. She had made a point of not learning any details about his profession, and he never spoke about business in front of her.

However, his eldest son, Ramón, took great pride in his father. Ramón was twenty-three years old and ran a smuggling ring in Bolivia as part of the "family business." One day he would inherit his father's throne, but El Tiburón knew his son still had much to learn, and he had no intention of retiring until he was sure he was too old to rule the roost. And that wouldn't be for a long time, he thought as he watched Major Pescador pace across the colorful handwoven rug in his office.

"I'm worried about possible conflicts between your men and my soldiers, El Tiburón," Major Pescador declared.

The coke czar cocked an eyebrow in surprise. "I don't understand."

"The values of your men are . . . a bad influence on my soldiers and the guerrilla fighters working with us."

"A bad influence?" El Tiburón laughed and shook his head.

Pescador was a major in the Cuban army, an intelligence officer and a devout Communist. His soldiers were expected to be loyal, blindly dedicated followers who would obey orders without question. Most were Cubans, but some were Sandinistas from Nicaragua. The "guerrilla fighters" were members of various terrorist organizations from Central and South America.

"There is nothing amusing about this matter, *señor*," Pescador said grimly. "Your men spend their off-duty hours watching television and movie videotapes. Many of these are American films. They also have a library of pornographic material. The refrigerators are stocked with rich, expensive foods. Your men even drink American-made whiskey and smoke American cigarettes...."

"So you want my men to lower their standard of living to keep your men from becoming envious?" El Tiburón smiled. "You're afraid we'll corrupt them and steer them away from the righteous cause of the revolution of the working class, eh?"

"We believe in the revolution," the Cuban said stiffly. "All you believe in is money. I don't mean to criticize, but your attitude is disturbing. It is similar to that of the capitalists to the north whom we are dedicated to oppose."

"Major," El Tiburón said with a sigh, "I admit my only real interest in cocaine is the profit involved. The people I work for are interested only in money and influence—which means power. This is the same goal your leaders are trying to achieve.''

"We are struggling to liberate the masses—'' Pescador began, thrusting a finger at the Bolivian gangster.

"Liberation?'' El Tiburón chuckled. "A Communist government does its best to control what its subjects read, hear, believe and think. The state owns the businesses and the media. It determines how goods will be produced and how services and products will be distributed. This has nothing to do with liberation. The so-called revolution is simply extending the tentacles of a Communist octopus that seeks more power over more individuals.''

"That is propaganda, the lies of our enemies,'' Pescador insisted, his moon face growing dark with anger.

"Politics doesn't interest me in the slightest, Major,'' El Tiburón told him. "Unless it concerns my business. The *norteamericanos* have a lot of money and I am glad they are my best customers. Frankly, I hope they continue to prosper, so they can buy more and more cocaine.''

"My superiors would be very upset by such remarks,'' Major Pescador said, shaking his head with dismay.

"They wouldn't be the least bit surprised,'' the Bolivian replied. "After all, one does not kill the goose that lays the eggs of gold. Many leaders of MERGE live in the United States. None of them would care to see communism take over their country. A number of them would be very upset if they knew we were doing business with you people."

"So the only reason you do business with us is because we help get the damned cocaine into the United States?" Pescador asked sadly. "You don't care that we do this because we hope to weaken and demoralize the *norteamericanos*?"

"I told you from the beginning that I don't give a damn what your reasons are," El Tiburón confessed. "Look, it isn't a state secret that your comrades, the Sandinistas, have refineries for processing cocaine in Nicaragua and that they help us get the drug into other Central American countries as well as Mexico and the U.S. The 'guerrilla fighters,' as you call them, have joined with us in growing coca plants and processing and distributing cocaine because the profits help finance their activities. And, of course, your grand comrades in the KGB have been involved in the heroin trade for years. There's even a heroin-processing plant near Sofia, Bulgaria, where narcotics are prepared for distribution to the United States and Western Europe."

"The decadent capitalists are simply being helped toward their own natural decay," Pescador declared.

"Of course," El Tiburón said dryly. He didn't feel like arguing with the Cuban. The Communists were involved in the dope traffic because it contributed to social unrest in Western democracies, but they also made a profit in the process. El Tiburón believed they weren't much different from the hoodlums in his own organization.

"Can't you discourage your men from indulging in those frivolous pastimes?" Pescador asked. "I don't want my men's virtue to be contaminated."

"Cuban soldiers in Angola are instructing SWAPO terrorists in torture techniques so that villagers who oppose communism can be punished and serve as an example to others," El Tiburón commented. "In Rhodesia, the Patriotic Front cut off the noses and lips of their victims. What sort of virtues are you endorsing these days?"

Major Pescador opened his mouth to reply, but El Tiburón cut him off by suddenly raising a hand.

"There's no point in arguing about this, Major," he insisted. "My men are not going to stop watching pornographic videotapes, smoking American cigarettes or eating steaks simply because these things make you worry about the Spartan dedication of your people. I haven't complained about the political lecturing that several of your followers indulge in. Especially that paratrooper Havana sent to instruct your guerrillas in personal combat."

"He happens to be a very dedicated soldier," the Cuban replied stiffly. "He believes entirely in the philosophy of Marx and Lenin, and he is devoted to the revolution."

"He's a fanatic, Major," the Bolivian stated. "A Marxist version of the zealots who carried out the

Holy Inquisition. I'd be careful of him, if I was in your position. He's crazy enough to turn against you if he suspects your heart is not pure enough for the cause of world communism.''

"The captain is a good man,'' Pescador insisted. "And he's my concern, not yours, El Tiburón.''

"He's currently attached to this operation.'' El Tiburón spoke slowly, emphatically. "*That* makes him my concern. You and your people are not in charge here, Major. I am. You've joined us because you have your own political and personal reasons. However, the cocaine trade is still my business—the business of El Dorado and the Colombian syndicate and MERGE. Without us, your people would get no more than a few kilos of cocaine into the United States.''

"Your authority is noted, *señor*,'' Pescador reluctantly admitted. He began to pace again. "I'll try to keep my men from associating with yours as long as they're in this area.''

"That's fine with me,'' El Tiburón assured him. "Now, our efforts to eliminate the narcotics agents and police enforcers who threaten our trade have worked quite well so far. The assassination of the enemy in Miami was the biggest success thus far. Miami is our most important port of entry for getting cocaine into the United States. We're going to concentrate on breaking down resistance there. If we can crush the DEA and the Miami vice squads, then we'll be able to ship more and more of the drug into the country.''

"Our agents in Miami will be ready to assist," Major Pescador promised. "When will the next strike take place?"

"Very soon," El Tiburón said with a smile. "I understand the police have already been fed the necessary information by misinformed flunkies who think they're going to set us up for a bust, as the *norteamericanos* say. But in reality, we're setting them up. Like sheep to be slaughtered."

"It's been easy so far," the Cuban said, nodding solemnly. "Perhaps *too* easy."

"Not for the sheep," El Tiburón said with a laugh.

5

"He's loose!" a uniformed cop shouted as he struggled with a large bearded man dressed in dirty, ragged clothing.

The five men of Phoenix Force saw the cop reach for his baton, but the bearded man grabbed the policeman and slammed him against the hood of the patrol car. Another cop already lay on the pavement, his stunned body squirming like a half-crushed insect. The bearded man pinned the second officer to the car and began hammering his face and head with a ham-sized fist.

"Jesus," Gary Manning rasped as he dashed across the street, closely followed by Rafael Encizo.

The pair managed to bolt to the other side of the street before traffic blocked the way for the rest of Phoenix Force and Lieutenant J. D. Leeper, the Miami vice cop assigned to work with the commando team. Manning and Encizo hurried to rescue the patrolman while the others watched for an opening in the procession of cars and trucks.

Manning was first to reach the shaggy hoodlum, who was still pounding away at the street cop's face. The guy raised his fist to strike the officer again. The Canadian's powerful hands suddenly grabbed the thug's arm, and at the same time he stamped a boot into the back of the man's knee. The bearded brute's leg folded, and Manning applied a straight-arm bar, pulling at the wrist and pushing above the elbow to lock the guy's arm.

"No!" the bearded man shrieked. "I must fly with the bats into the limbo of the night!"

He struggled violently. The guy was big, but so was Gary Manning. The Canadian was in superb physical condition, a long-distance runner, weight lifter and expert in judo and jujitsu. Yet Manning was having a lot of trouble holding on to his berserk opponent. Encizo reached for the guy's other arm to help Manning subdue the ranting brute.

The man slammed his left forearm into Encizo. The force knocked the Cuban backward into the patrol car. Manning increased the pressure of his arm lock, but the guy struggled harder. Bone cracked in the berserker's right elbow. He didn't seem to notice as he thrust his head forward and butted his skull into Manning's chest. The Canadian staggered, and the lunatic broke free of the hold.

"Demons!" the bearded man howled, his right arm dangling useless at his side. "I am the light of the universe! You think you can stop me? Fuck—"

Encizo hit him in the side of the neck, chopping the edge of his hand into the nerve center. The blow would have rendered most men unconscious, but the wild-eyed brute whirled and smashed the back of his left fist into Encizo's face. The Cuban tumbled to the pavement.

Manning rammed his fist into the point of his opponent's chin. The punch would have knocked the average man unconscious, but the guy's head simply recoiled from the blow. His body didn't budge. Manning hit him again with a left hook. Teeth spewed from the berserker's mouth. He still didn't go down. Instead, he swung his left fist into the Canadian's face. Manning stumbled backward from the blow and nearly staggered into the path of an oncoming taxi.

"Bastard spawn of Satan!" the rampaging hulk cried.

Rafael Encizo had risen from the ground and snap-kicked the man in the gut. The wacko barely grunted. Encizo punched him in the side of the head. The blow barely fazed the guy. He swung his left fist at Encizo. The Cuban blocked the attack with a forearm and hit his opponent with a solid left jab.

Blood oozed from the madman's broken nose, but he didn't seem to feel pain or care that he had been hit. His left hand grabbed at Encizo's face as if trying to rip his features to ribbons. The Cuban dodged the clawing fingers and swung a right cross to the brute's jaw.

Manning attacked the berserk hood from behind. He seized the guy's collar and rammed a knee into the weirdo's tailbone. The kick forced the wild man into the frame of the car. Manning slapped him in the back of the skull, bashing the guy's forehead into the auto's steel frame.

Encizo helped Manning shove the freak against the car. The Cuban raised his arm and slammed a hard karate chop behind his opponent's left ear. Then he hit him again. The bearded man finally stopped struggling and started to sag. Manning took a white plastic strip from his pocket and quickly bound the man's wrists together behind his back.

"Bloody hell!" McCarter shouted as he jogged across the street. The traffic had finally thinned enough to allow the others to cross. "You sure this bloke isn't an android from another planet or something?"

"PCP freak," Encizo said breathlessly as they shoved the man to the ground. The Cuban bound the guy's ankles together with another set of riot cuffs.

"Look at this," Manning commented, pointing at the steel bracelets locked around the man's wrists. Metal links dangled from each band. "The cops had already cuffed the bastard, but he broke the chain."

"I'm not really surprised," Encizo replied, rubbing his bruised jaw. "He hit like a truck. And we just about had to hit *him* with a truck to bring him down."

Another patrol car pulled up to the curb. Two uniformed cops bounded from the vehicle and drew service revolvers. Lieutenant Leeper marched to the pair and flapped open his ID folder to show them his badge.

"Put those guns away, damn it," Leeper snapped. "The situation is under control now. They call you guys in for backup?"

"Uh...yes, sir," one of the patrolmen answered with a nervous nod. He tried three times before successfully returning his revolver to its holster.

"Where the hell have you been?" Leeper demanded. "Two cops nearly got killed because this PCP psycho broke his cuffs and turned on them."

"Look, Lieutenant," the older of the two patrolmen replied in a weary voice, "you know we're undermanned. My partner and I were hauling in a couple of kids who'd ripped off a liquor store when we got the call. Fuckin' junior junkies. I don't think either of them is more than fifteen years old. We were taking them to the station house—"

"Okay, okay," Leeper cut him off. "Call an ambulance. We have two injured officers here and a suspect who probably has a dozen broken bones he'll be aware of when he comes down from the angel dust. Okay?"

"Affirmative, Lieutenant," the senior cop said. "These guys with you as part of a stakeout...or shouldn't I ask?"

"They're invisible," Leeper told him. "You didn't see them and you can't see them now. Understand?"

"Not really," the cop admitted. "But I hear you."

"Good," Leeper replied. "Write down your names and badge numbers for me. There's a good reason why you guys should keep your mouths shut about this. If you keep a lid on it, I'll see that the department shows you some consideration. If you open your mouths, I'll see if I can't arrange something appropriate for that, too."

"How long will that lid have to stay on?" the cop asked.

"A week," Leeper assured him. "No more, no less. All I can tell you is it concerns the Feds. Special Feds. Not DEA."

"Okay, Lieutenant Leeper," the cop assured him. He used the lieutenant's last name to let Leeper know he could nail him if the lid turned out to be hiding something rotten.

"Fair enough," Leeper said with a nod.

Calvin James, the Phoenix Force medic, had been examining the two police officers who had been overpowered by the drug-crazed man. He turned to Leeper.

"Both of these dudes have some facial bone damage and one has a broken jaw," James told him. "Temples, orbital bones, glabella, sphenoid all seem to be intact. Probably got concussions, but I think they'll be okay. Their dentists are sure gonna make a bundle." The black warrior knelt beside the dazed PCP user to examine his injuries.

Manning rubbed a bruised knuckle and shook his head. "Does this sort of thing happen very often, Lieutenant?" he inquired.

"You wouldn't believe how often," Leeper said grimly. "I'd say at least two-thirds of all crime in Miami is connected one way or another with drugs."

Leeper shrugged, accepting the helplessness of his situation. He appeared to be in his mid-thirties, with the lean physique of an athlete. The slightly tinted, oval-shaped lenses of his glasses concealed some of the weariness in his eyes, and a well-tailored sport jacket hid most of the bulge of the Colt .357 Magnum under his arm.

"This sucker's in worse shape than the two cops he beat up," Calvin James announced as he looked up from beside the PCP freak. "Nose, jawbone, several teeth, his right elbow and about half the bones in both hands appear to be broken. A number of tendons in his wrists are pulled out of place. A couple snapped like rubber bands. His shoulder is also dislocated. Even though he's unconscious, his heartbeat sounds like a Buddy Rich concert. This dude is gonna be in bad shape for a long time."

"He's still in better shape than a hell of a lot of junkies I see every day," Leeper stated. "Come on, we'd better get moving if we're going to keep our appointment."

The men of Phoenix Force followed Leeper as he threaded his way back through the traffic to the parking lot they had been approaching when they'd seen the disturbance across the street. Katz and McCarter got into Leeper's Renault Alliance. Encizo got behind the wheel of a Toyota Corolla he had rented at Miami International Airport, and opened the passenger doors for Manning and James. The Cuban had spent several years in Miami and knew the city well.

They drove to Flagler Street and cut across town, heading for Biscayne Boulevard. Downtown Miami was ablaze with pulsating red and orange neon. Temptation to pleasures of the flesh lurked on almost every block. Bars, nightclubs and porno shops were plentiful. Streetwalkers paraded the sidewalks.

Less blatant but just as plentiful were the pushers who patrolled the district. If you could swallow it, snort it, smoke it or shoot it into your veins, there was someone in the neon jungle who would sell it to you. The street dealers were the little fish that kept the big fish in business. And business would go on as long as the demand for the product existed.

"You know, ninety years ago Miami had a population of 343," Leeper commented as he put two sticks of chewing gum in his mouth and steered the Renault past the Miamarina. "Hard to believe 'cause now we've got close to two million, not including eleven or twelve million tourists every year."

"Well, it's a beautiful city," Yakov Katzenelenbogen remarked, "though a bit flashy for my taste. Reminds me a bit of Las Vegas. An adult Disneyland."

"Yeah," Leeper agreed. "But we've also got concerts, ballet, theater. If you're into sports, we've got the Orange Bowl, and jai alai at the Fronton, not to mention one of the best zoos in the world. Got a couple white Bengal tigers there. Even the San Diego Zoo can't claim that."

"I'm afraid we won't have time for sight-seeing this trip," Katz replied, smoothing out the pearl-gray glove that covered his artificial hand. The device wasn't as versatile as the hooked prosthesis, but it attracted less attention.

"You know, I wasn't told who you guys really are," Leeper remarked as they drove up Biscayne Boulevard. Palm trees and goosenecked streetlamps lined the curb. "If you were regular DEA agents, you'd have arrived with the other Feds last week. It seemed a little strange, to me, to be ordered out to the airport to pick up five guys on a special government airplane, who can shuffle past customs without even going through a metal detector."

"We're a bit unorthodox," David McCarter said with a shrug.

"I don't think you're DEA, either," Leeper commented. "But you're not gonna tell me anyway, so the hell with it."

"I think it's fair to tell you why you were chosen to pick us up, Lieutenant," Katz said. "We needed somebody from the Miami vice squad we could trust. Somebody who couldn't be bought off by the coke dealers. You were selected."

"Well, it's nice to be trusted." Leeper smiled. "And since you need somebody you can trust, that means you're worried about dirty cops in the department."

"I'm sorry to say that's correct," Katz confirmed.

"The lousy thing is it doesn't surprise me," Leeper said. "A couple of years ago, the county realized we were short on manpower. Between the dope trade, the *marielitos* and the usual thieves and murderers, we were goddamn swamped. So they started hiring more cops. The new guys were screened, but not very well. Just about anybody who applied got on the force. A few of 'em turned out to have criminal records as long as your arm. Unfortunately, we've had more than our share of cops on the take."

"That's not necessarily the case this time," Mc-Carter told the vice cop. "It could just be that somebody's setting up you chaps with false information."

"Christ!" Leeper rasped. "You must be talking about what happened to Martinez and his group. You mean, we're going for another bust that'll really be an ambush?"

"We're going with you just in case that happens," Katz assured him. "Just in case."

"Terrific," Leeper muttered. "You know, the goddamn Colombians, or whoever was responsible, dropped a barrel of homemade napalm on Martinez's group from the belly of a plane."

"Gasoline, motor oil, soap flakes with some sort of incendiary device, possibly a road flare," Katz declared. "A crude firebomb, but effective."

"Effective enough to roast a dozen guys," Leeper remarked. "I figure you fellas brought some impressive firepower in those crates you hauled off the plane. Maybe some high-tech stuff, too. Heat sensors, laser microphones with infinity amplifiers and special night-vision gear. But don't forget, the Colombian syndicate and the other crime outfits in the cocaine trade made billions of dollars with nose candy. They can afford to buy a lot of fancy weapons, gadgets and gizmos, too, and people who know how to use all of the above."

McCarter grinned. "Like I said before, we're a bit unorthodox. So are our methods, mate."

"I just hope they work," the vice cop said, shaking his head.

LESS THAN HALF AN HOUR later, Phoenix Force and Lieutenant Leeper joined Harold Krebs and several other DEA agents and Miami vice cops in a safehouse in an upper-middle-class neighborhood on Biscayne Boulevard. The split-level ranch-style dwelling was used occasionally for the federal protected-witness program. High muck-a-mucks in the crime world were accustomed to living well and were apt to have second thoughts about cooperating if forced to hole up in a fleabag hotel.

"Glad to see everybody could make it," Krebs began, nodding at the men of Phoenix Force. "I think we all know what the plan is, but I want everybody to meet everybody else, so if there's any shooting, we won't pump bullets into the wrong person.''

Krebs scratched his balding pate and pointed at a window. "Out there is Biscayne Bay," he announced. "There's yachts and houseboats and assorted pleasure craft out there. It's a fun place for water sports. Tomorrow night, according to a reliable source, there'll be a garbage scow puttering along out there. It'll eventually stop at Pier Fourteen, where the crew will dig into the trash on board and produce approximately one hundred kilos of Bolivian marching powder. I don't have to tell anyone in this room that a hundred kilos is worth at least a couple of million dollars.''

"They'll have some guns guarding that much coke," a wiry blond detective called Ronald Johnson commented, puffing on a cigarette. "Probably packin' automatic weapons.''

"We'll have automatic weapons, too," DEA agent Frank Paris declared. He was a big guy, built like a football lineman, and unaccustomed to worrying about threats from lesser mortals.

"Martinez and his group had automatic weapons," Detective Carlos M. Phillips reminded the DEA agent. Phillips was a mulatto with a rich coffee-and-cream complexion. "Didn't do them much good.''

"I figure the smugglers saw the stakeout from the air," another vice cop called Burgess Polaski remarked with a shrug. He scratched his unkempt black beard and added, "We'll be in a better position to conceal ourselves than they were."

"I got a question," a short DEA agent with a bald bullet-shaped head said. His name was Albert Gross, and his small squinty eyes were trained on Phoenix Force. "Who the fuck are these guys? Nobody told us this was gonna be a goddamn national conference. If we bring along anybody else, the fuckin' pier will give way under our weight."

McCarter shrugged. "Too bad we don't have time to go on a crash diet."

"Just don't wear any heavy jewelry," Calvin James suggested.

"Is there any special reason you object to us being present?" Katz asked the DEA man.

"Yeah, two reasons," Gross answered. "First is, if we have too many people at the stakeout, the smugglers are gonna spot us before they make the deal. We might get blown away like Martinez's stakeout. The other reason is, I don't know you guys. I don't like working with people I don't know."

"And people who know you aren't too crazy about working with you," Johnson muttered as he crushed the cigarette in a glass ashtray.

"Amen," Phillips added with a grin.

"Who gives a shit what you think?" Gross snapped. "Do you know these guys, Leeper?"

"Just met them tonight," the lieutenant said. "They seem to know what they're doing. Thought they were your men, Harry."

"They're attached to another group," Krebs answered. "I'll vouch for them. Any problem with that, Gross?"

"Just like to know who I'm workin' with, sir," Gross replied, but his beady eyes still inspected Phoenix Force with suspicion.

"So long as they're Feds," Agent Paris remarked, cracking his knuckles, "it's okay with me."

"What's that suppose to mean?" Polaski demanded. The bearded vice cop was almost as big as Paris and obviously not intimidated by the DEA agent. "If you got some doubts about working with the Miami PD on this, why don't you just sing right out?"

"All I'm saying is you've got some crooked cops on the force," Paris answered. He met Polaski's stare and locked eyes with the vice cop. "I'd hate to have one of 'em behind me in a shoot-out."

"How'd you like to take your teeth home in a doggie bag?" Polaski growled, balling his fists as he approached.

"Come on, big mouth," Paris invited, wiggling his fingers to goad the vice cop into taking the first swing.

"That's enough!" Krebs ordered.

"That goes for both of you," Leeper added.

"When this is over..." Polaski told Paris, stepping away from the DEA agent with a scowl.

"You've got it, asshole," Paris replied with a nod.

"Any more schoolboy crap and you're both bounced," Krebs warned. "God knows, the smugglers will give us enough to worry about without us fighting among ourselves.''

Yakov Katzenelenbogen fished a pack of Camels from his pocket and shook a cigarette loose. He caught it in his lips and pulled it from the pack. McCarter had also gotten out his Player's and offered a light to Katz.

"What do you think so far?" the Briton whispered.

"I've worked with teams I've had more confidence in," the Phoenix Force commander replied softly. "Leeper seems competent. I'm not so sure about the others."

"We'd better just count on ourselves," Encizo suggested. "Business as usual."

"Well, thank God for that," James muttered. "I hate it when stuff happens I'm not prepared for."

6

Moonlight shimmered on the choppy waves of Biscayne Bay. The night was unseasonably chilly. Tourists, yacht owners and even bold fishermen chose to stay indoors and away from the water.

This suited Phoenix Force and the other members of the stakeout team. They didn't want to have to worry about civilians in the area. The five commandos and their DEA and vice squad allies waited among the shadows beyond Pier Fourteen and watched for the garbage scow to arrive.

Phoenix Force had split up. Katz, McCarter and Encizo waited with Leeper and the vice cops in a bait shop near the pier. James and Manning were with Harold Krebs and his DEA agents, stationed in a nondescript motel less than a block away. Agent Gross peered through an infrared telescope trained on Pier Fourteen. The bald, pig-eyed DEA man frequently glanced over his shoulder to check on Manning and James.

Gary Manning had assembled an FAL assault rifle with a Starlite scope mounted to the frame. The Canadian pro also carried an Eagle .357 Magnum auto-loader in shoulder leather. Calvin James was armed with an M-16 assault rifle with a 50-round extended magazine and an M-203 grenade launcher attached under the barrel. He packed a .45 caliber Colt Commander in a Jackass Leather rig, with the pistol holstered under his left arm and a G-96 Jet-Aer dagger in a sheath under his right.

As soon as they entered the motel room the two Phoenix Force warriors had exchanged their street clothes for black night-camouflage uniforms. The DEA agents were startled when they saw that the pair had donned combat attire and unpacked enough firepower to take on a busload of opponents.

"I thought you fellas understood that we plan to arrest the coke smugglers," Agent Paris remarked, "not shoot the shit out of them."

"We don't usually arrest people," Calvin James replied. "If the enemy gives up without a battle, then you dudes can have the collar."

"And if the smugglers don't surrender?" Gross inquired, glaring at James as if daring him to make a snotty response.

"Then we'll shoot the shit out of them," the black guy answered simply. "Kind of a specialty of ours. Know what I mean?"

"Did you hear that, Mr. Krebs?" Paris asked.

Krebs sighed. "Unfortunately, I did."

"And you're still going to let them stay here as part of the stakeout?" Paris demanded.

"That's right," Krebs said wearily. "I told you before, I'll vouch for these men."

"Have they had their rabies shots?" Gross muttered sourly.

"You don't really understand what we do," Manning told the DEA agents. He slid a magazine into his FAL, chambered a round and switched the selector to the "safe" position. "We're used as a last resort when a situation calls for it. But we're professionals. We don't use a battle ax when a situation calls for a tack hammer."

"Or the other way around," James added. "You guys are wearing gray suits, white shirts and ties. You've got Fed written all over you. The hoods are gonna make you guys the second you get close to the pier."

"Look, wiseass," Gross growled, "we're law-enforcement officers, not undercover vice cops. The Miami fuzz handle that. They know the local scene better than us. Better than you. That's why they're undercover down at the bait shop and we're backin' them up."

"Yeah," James replied, "this is safer."

"What the fuck!" Gross growled. "You guys play Rambo for a living? I don't believe it—"

"We do our job as well or better than you fellows do," Manning announced in a hard voice. "Frankly, I don't see why you're all dressed like bank executives for a stakeout. Do you want to look nice when the press shows up with their cameras?"

"Now, wait a minute—" Paris began.

"We've listened to you," Manning cut in. "Shut up and listen to us for a minute. I've noticed this before. Police worry too much about their 'on screen image,' but you Feds are even worse. I know times when federal officers have been killed, or gotten someone else killed, because they hesitated to hit the dirt when the shooting started. They didn't want to get their suits messed up."

"Hey!" Krebs said with annoyance. "Ease up on my men."

"We're talking to you, too, Harry," James informed him. "We're far enough from the pier that none of us will reach the smugglers before the vice cops and our partners who are with them. But none of you dudes have a rifle. You three are carrying snub-nosed revolvers that are useless in a firefight unless you get in close. By the time we get close, our friends could be dead, man."

"I've got a shotgun," Paris announced, jerking a thumb toward the twelve-gauge pump propped against a corner.

"Shotgun is fine if you can get close enough to use it," Manning stated. "Same problem. I know I sound more critical than I have a right to be. After all, you gentlemen aren't trained to act as shock troops. You're taught to locate narcotics being smuggled into the country, to recognize and analyze drugs. You study laws and smuggling techniques and gather evidence for arrests. But they don't teach you enough about what

to do when the intended quarry turns on you and tries to kill you."

"Give me a break," Gross snarled. "We qualify with firearms and take a course in combat shooting."

"Yeah," James stated. "But you're trained to defend yourselves against pretty much equal odds. It's assumed that you'll outnumber the opponents and that they'll be armed with handguns, maybe shotguns or machine pistols. But the situation has changed since 1975. The guys behind the cocaine traffic are making billions of dollars. They can hire small armies of gunmen and equip them with everything short of nuclear weapons. And they've got contract killers. Anyone who specializes in just one thing gets to be pretty good at it."

"Speaking from personal experience?" Paris sneered.

"To a degree," James admitted. "We're not murderers, but we don't hesitate to kill if it's necessary."

"Well," Gross said gruffly, "you can save part of that lecture because the cops have a couple of SWAT snipers on the roof. They'll handle any long-range shooting, probably do a better job at it than you guys would. Although you might find it hard to believe anyone can do anything better than you."

"That depends on what you're talking about," Manning said with a shrug. But before he finished his sentence, Paris picked up his shotgun and aimed it at the big Canadian.

LIEUTENANT LEEPER, Detective Polaski and two SWAT cops were inside the bait shop with the other three members of Phoenix Force. Unlike the DEA agents with Manning and James, none of the Miami cops wore suits. Leeper wore a black turtleneck sweater with dark trousers and an old U.S. Army field jacket. Polaski was clad in dark gray work clothes and a brown leather jacket. The SWAT cops had entered the shop earlier that evening, dressed in street clothes and carrying military duffel bags. They had changed into dark blue uniforms with matching baseball caps. The Phoenix pros wore black camies for the occasion.

Leeper and Lieutenant Ramón Garfalo, the SWAT team commander, were armed with CAR-15 automatic carbines. Polaski and the other SWAT cop had shotguns. The Phoenix Force trio were glad to see the police at the stakeout were armed with more than service revolvers.

The cops were impressed by the weaponry carried by the Phoenix warriors, although the three had fewer arms than usual for a mission. Yakov Katzenelenbogen had an Uzi submachine gun and a 9 mm SIG-Sauer P-226 pistol in a shoulder holster under his right arm. McCarter carried his favorite weapons—an Ingram M-10 machine pistol and a Browning Hi-Power automatic, both 9 mm parabellum. Rafael Encizo was packing even more hardware—a Heckler & Koch MP-5 machine pistol, a 9 mm Smith & Wesson Model 59 on his hip and a .380 caliber Walther PPK in shoul-

der leather. In addition, Encizo had a large Cold Steel Tanto knife on his belt and a Gerber Mark I fighting dagger in a boot sheath.

"Why the knives, amigo?" Garfalo inquired when he noticed the Cuban's blades.

"They've saved my life more than once," the Cuban replied with a smile.

Detective Johnson and Carlos Phillips, the mulatto vice cop, were stationed in the back of a flower delivery van near the bait shop. The van was equipped with a rifle microphone and an infrared periscope. Leeper communicated with the pair and with Harold Krebs on a walkie-talkie.

"Hey, Lieutenant!" Johnson's voice came over Leeper's two-way radio. "There's some guys walkin' around on the pier. At least three men who appear to be armed with compact weapons hanging from shoulder straps. Probably machine pistols."

"What about the scow?" Leeper asked, speaking into the walkie-talkie.

"No sign of her yet," Johnson answered. "Let us know if you decide to pull out."

"Pull out, hell," Phillips put in after Johnson's remark. "At least we can bust those guys on the pier."

"Don't do *anything* unless I give you the okay," Leeper insisted.

"Understood, Lieutenant." Phillips sighed.

"Don't lose your temper," Leeper warned. "That's the way to make mistakes, and we can't afford any. Keep in touch."

Leeper switched off the radio. He turned to Katz. "Phillips is itching to get his hands on some major drug dealers," the vice cop explained. "But if he can't get a big one, he'll settle for a street pusher. He's got a personal commitment to that goal."

"Do you mean an emotional commitment?" Katz asked.

"Sort of," Leeper confirmed. "Last week a little kid was murdered by some junkies. They smashed his head in with a pop bottle full of sand. Homicide couldn't figure it out since the kid had money in his pocket. They investigated the boy's background. Came from a poor family. Four other kids in the home and the mother's a single parent, working her ass off to pay the rent and take care of the children. Well, the boy had found a way to get more money."

"Some pusher recruited the kid to use as a mule?" Rafael Encizo guessed.

"That's right," Leeper said with a nod. "Dealers use kids to deliver dope to clients, or move the shit from one site to another when they figure a hiding place is getting too hot. A little kid is an ideal mule. He has only a vague idea of what cocaine and heroin are. Give him ten bucks to deliver a hundred thousand worth in dope, and the kid thinks he's getting a good deal. An eight-year-old from a ghetto can't even imagine how much a hundred grand is."

"And who would suspect a child was carrying dope in his lunch box?" Encizo added.

"Ghetto kids don't trust the police," Leeper remarked. "Most of them figure we'll throw them in jail."

"Maybe that's where they belong." Polaski snorted.

"Put eight-year-old children in a federal prison?" McCarter glared at Polaski. "What would you accomplish? Make bleedin' sure they'll be criminals by the age of sixteen?"

"Some of them don't live that long," Encizo said grimly.

"What sort of a bastard would use children to carry dope?" the Briton said with a frown.

"A greedy bastard," Leeper stated. "You won't find any morals or principles among dope dealers. If a pusher had a blind grandmother in a wheelchair, he'd use her for a mule if he thought it would work."

"Just another way that narcotics ruins people's lives," Encizo said grimly. "Nothing new about sons of bitches exploiting others and making personal gain from human suffering. That's been happening for centuries, and it'll probably continue as long as there are people."

Leeper's walkie-talkie crackled with static, and a new voice spoke from the radio.

"This is Krebs," the DEA agent announced. "We just spotted a boat approaching the pier. I think it's the garbage scow. Hope you guys are ready."

"So do I," Leeper replied. "Take care of yourselves."

Leeper radioed Johnson and Phillips in the van to inform them of Krebs's report, while Lieutenant Garfalo used another walkie-talkie to alert his SWAT team. McCarter attached a nine-inch noise suppressor to the threaded barrel of his Browning pistol. Katz had already attached a silencer to his SIG-Sauer.

Encizo peered out a window. The glass was blurred and smudged, the pier dimly lit, yet he could see the lights of the garbage scow as it docked. Shadowy figures approached the boat, and someone at the bow tossed a line to one of them.

"Looks like it's going down," Leeper remarked as he joined Encizo at the window. The vice cop clipped an ID badge with his gold shield on the lapel of his jacket. "You guys tagged? Hate for you to get shot by one of our people who didn't realize you're on our side."

"We've got the badges," Encizo replied. "But we won't put them on until we're sure they won't jeopardize us."

"How's that?" Leeper asked.

"Shiny metal reflects light," the Cuban answered. "If we try to creep up on these jokers in the dark, we don't want to wear something that will flash the instant the moonlight strikes it."

"Good point," the vice cop admitted.

Leeper glanced over his shoulder and noticed that Detective Polaski had pulled on a pair of tan driver's gloves. The police lieutenant wondered why the gloves. Then he saw Polaski gather up his riot gun. The vice cop turned sharply, his back to the wall, and pointed the shotgun at Leeper and Encizo.

Holy shit, the lieutenant thought. Before he could utter his thoughts, let alone reach for the revolver under his arm, something slammed into him and knocked him off his feet. For a split second, Leeper wondered if he had been shot without hearing the gun roar. Then he realized Encizo had bowled him over. The Cuban had thrown himself into the vice cop to send both men to the floor.

Leeper gazed up at Polaski as the treacherous detective dropped his shotgun and fell backward. His body slid down the wall to the floor. Two bullet holes in his forehead and left temple oozed small trickles of blood. Considerably more blood and gray brain matter had spewed from the larger exit wounds at the back of his skull.

Yakov Katzenelenbogen and David McCarter held their silencer-equipped pistols, still aimed at the lifeless form of Detective Polaski. Smoke curled from the muzzles of the sound suppressors.

"Sweet Jesus," Lieutenant Garfalo rasped, fumbling for the service revolver on his hip.

"No!" Leeper shouted to the SWAT cop. "Polaski was about to kill me. I saw him point the shotgun just before our friends took him out."

"Garfalo," Katz said sharply, "contact your officers and tell them they're in danger."

"What?" The SWAT commander glared at him. "You've got some explaining to do...."

"We've been set up," Katz replied. "The enemy is going to try to kill us. Now, tell your men somebody is going to attack them."

"Polaski knew about the SWAT team," Encizo added.

"Shit!" Garfalo reached for his walkie-talkie.

"You guys don't seem very surprised this happened," Leeper commented, glancing at the faces of the three Phoenix Force members.

"We knew what happened to Lieutenant Martinez and his group," Katz said with a nod. "And we suspected it might happen again."

"And you suspected Polaski was working for the smugglers?" the vice cop asked.

"There isn't time for explanations," McCarter warned as he gathered up his Ingram M-10. "Better contact Johnson and Phillips to tell them the hunters have become the hunted."

7

Calvin James saw Agent Paris pump the action of his shotgun and aim the Winchester blaster at Gary Manning. The black warrior bolted forward and slammed a forearm to the shotgun barrel. He forced the muzzle toward the ceiling. Paris pulled the trigger.

The bellow of the shotgun filled the motel room. Buckshot smashed a large hole in the ceiling. Plaster dust rained down on James and Paris as they struggled with the shotgun. Harold Krebs and Albert Gross were motionless in shock, but Manning barely glanced at the struggling pair. The Canadian swung his FAL rifle toward the door.

It suddenly burst open, the flimsy lock broken by a hard kick. Two men appeared at the threshold. Both wore cheap raincoats and carried compact Ingram M-11 machine pistols, the .380 caliber version of the MAC-10. Hats with wide brims concealed some of their features, but their olive complexion suggested they might be Hispanic.

Gary Manning didn't care what ethnic group the gunmen belonged to. He didn't discriminate. When someone threatened his life, Manning would kill the guy regardless of his race, creed or national origin. He opened fire before the enemy could trigger their Ingram room cleaners.

Manning's first round nailed the closest opponent somewhere between the brim of his hat and the collar of his raincoat. The high velocity 7.62 mm slug punched through the killer's face, sliced a tunnel in his brain and tore out a chunk of skull at the back of his head. The gunman's body collapsed in the hallway, the unfired machine pistol still clenched in his fists.

The other gunman tried to point his Ingram at Manning, but the Canadian swiftly aimed from the hip and fired. The moving target was a bit luckier than his comrade. Manning's bullet hit him high in the chest. The FAL round missed the sternum, ripped through body tissue as it traveled upward to blast an exit wound under the guy's right shoulder. If the assault rifle had been switched on full-auto, the man's chest would have become bloodied hamburger. Instead, the single 7.62 mm messenger caused enough damage to render the man's right arm useless. The Ingram slipped from his fingers.

The gunman staggered down the corridor, dazed and injured but still on his feet. Manning stepped to the doorway, FAL still pointed at the attacker. Other doors opened and motel residents peeked out from their rooms. When they saw Manning's rifle, the curious guests retreated hastily and shut their doors.

Although stunned and wounded, the gunman reached for a pistol in his belt. His right arm hung slack from his wrecked shoulder, and his left hand fumbled at the butt of his backup piece.

"Give it up!" Manning warned, putting the stock of his FAL to his shoulder in order to aim precisely at the gunman's head.

The hit man stared into the muzzle of Manning's weapon and realized his situation was hopeless. He used two fingers to pull the pistol from his belt and dropped it to the floor. He raised his left arm in surrender.

Calvin James was still struggling with Agent Paris. The shotgun was a threat, although the pump would have to be jacked to chamber another shell, but James was more concerned about the DEA agent's snub-nosed revolver. If Paris could hold James at bay long enough to draw his piece, the black warrior would have his guts ventilated by at least one .38 slug.

James shoved the shotgun into his opponent, holding it like a bar against his chest. He stomped a boot heel into Paris's instep and hooked the front of a bent elbow into the agent's jawbone. Paris groaned, and James quickly chopped a forearm across the man's wrists. The shotgun clattered to the floor.

A backfist stroke caught Paris in the center of the face, breaking the cartilage at the bridge of his nose. James turned slightly and rammed an elbow into the guy's solar plexus. Paris started to fold from the blow, but he was a big man and just as tough as he looked.

Paris suddenly swung a short uppercut at James's chin. The black man's head bounced from the punch, and Paris lashed out with a left hook. The fist rushed past the tip of James's nose as he dodged the punch and jabbed his own left under the larger man's breastbone.

James followed with a solid right cross to his opponent's jaw. Paris staggered against the wall, but was still on his feet. His fingers pawed at the grips of the revolver under his arm. James kicked him in the balls. Paris uttered an ugly animal sound and wilted to the floor.

"What the fuck is goin' on?" Agent Gross asked, confused. The bullet-headed DEA agent had drawn his revolver, but held his fire, not sure what had happened.

"Paris tried to off us," James answered as he took the traitor's revolver from its holster and tossed the piece to Krebs. "And he had a couple of chums for backup."

"Paris was working for the Colombians?" Krebs inquired, shaken by the incident.

"We don't know if we're up against the Colombian syndicate or some other outfit," Manning replied as he shoved the wounded gunman into the room. "But whoever they are, Paris and this asshole were on their payroll."

"I know we discussed the possibility that the drug czars had spies in the DEA and the Miami police,"

Krebs remarked. "But I didn't think we'd have one of 'em at the stakeout."

"Yeah," Gross added. "And who would have suspected Paris after he and that big Polack nearly got in a fistfight 'cause the bastard had the nerve to imply there were crooks on the Miami vice squad."

"Actually, that made me suspicious," Manning stated. "Those two were acting like punk street kids, yet both are experienced law-enforcement officers. Why would Paris and Polaski behave like immature adolescents, making accusations and silly threats?"

"I was kinda rough on you guys," Gross reminded them. "Why weren't you suspicious of me?"

"Who said we weren't?" James replied with a grin as he bound Paris's wrists at the small of his back with plastic riot cuffs. "We had to be suspicious of everybody. Even you, Harry."

"That's nice," Krebs growled.

"That's just the way things are," James said with a shrug. "Trusting people isn't part of our job. But we were especially suspicious of Paris and Polaski because they behaved like such shitheads. Throwing accusations and stupid challenges was probably meant to convince us of their dedication, but it was unprofessional and sounded a bit too deliberate."

"That means Polaski could be a spy too!" Krebs reached for his walkie-talkie.

"Our partners are with Leeper's group," Manning stated. "They'll keep an eye on Polaski and the other cops. The real threat will come from the enemy at the pier and probably from other opponents who'll hit us from the rear.''

"Those SWAT cops on the roof are in danger," James, a former SWAT cop himself, warned. "So are the others stationed in the area."

"You want to check on the cops on the roof?" Manning asked. "I'll go outside to help the others with the guys at the pier."

"Okay," James agreed, reaching for his M-16.

"Harry," Manning said as he headed for the door, "you keep an eye on Paris and the other prisoner. Somebody's probably called the police about the shooting already, but make sure they're on the way and warn them how dangerous the situation is. We don't want the cops to get picked off as soon as they get out of the squad cars."

"You're giving orders now?" Krebs frowned, then said with a shrug, "The hell with it, you guys seem to know what you're doing. Watch yourselves out there."

"We intend to," James replied, following Manning out the door.

"Hey!" Agent Gross exclaimed as he rushed forward. "I'm going with you guys."

Manning had already reached the stairs and bounded down the steps to the lobby below. James headed for a ladder to the roof, slinging his M-16 over his shoulder so as to have both hands free. Gross followed the black commando up the rungs of the ladder.

James drew his Colt Commander. As he shoved up the trapdoor that opened onto the roof, the unoiled hinges creaked. Two men dressed in windbreakers and chinos stood with their backs to James. At the sound of the creaking hinges, they whipped around, silencer-equipped pistols in their fists.

The swarthy men with hard black eyes weren't SWAT cops, and that was all James needed to know. His Colt Commander blasted a 185-grain hollow-point round into the solar plexus of the nearest gunman. The bullet ripped upward into the hoodlum's heart. The force hurled the man backward, the life crushed from his body.

The second gunman swung his 9 mm Beretta toward James, but he wasn't quick enough. James fired his Commander and emerged from the trapdoor with a quick shoulder roll onto the roof. The gunman cried out, a .45 caliber slug burrowing into his intestines. He doubled up in agony, but still managed to pull the trigger of his Beretta. A parabellum round sizzled past James's tumbling form. The Phoenix pro felt the projectile tug at his pant leg. A sharp pain lanced his calf.

The hit man still held on to his gun and tried to aim it at James. The black dude from the Windy City rolled on his belly, his Colt pistol held in a two-handed Weaver grip. He pumped two rounds into the chest of his opponent. The gunman spun around from the impact of the heavy .45 slugs and fell to all fours. He tried feebly to crawl, then collapsed on his face and died.

Suddenly James glimpsed another man approaching from the right, the snout of a machine pistol jutting from the box-shaped M-10 in the man's fists. James quickly retreated behind the insubstantial cover of the trapdoor. A salvo of 9 mm rounds raked his position. High-velocity bullets splintered the flimsy door and pierced the tarred skin of the roof. James sprawled behind the door while the projectiles sizzled above his prone body.

He was pinned down. He couldn't shoot back without exposing himself to the deadly hailstorm of automatic fire. Yet he couldn't stay put and let the machine gunner rip away his ineffective cover. The Phoenix fighter had no choice. He swallowed his fear and prepared to make his move—aware that it would probably be his last.

The bellow of a Magnum handgun interrupted the metallic chatter of the gunman's M-10. James saw the hit man's body recoil, then convulse in a bizarre backward shuffle toward the edge of the roof. The guy still held his Ingram blaster, but he fired the remaining rounds into the night sky. Crimson stains spread over his torso.

James aimed his .45 and fired into the wounded man. The big round knocked the hood over the lip of the roof, and he plunged three stories to the pavement below.

Albert Gross climbed through the opening of the trapdoor. Smoke still curled from the barrel of the snub-nosed .357 Magnum in his fist. James unslung his M-16 from his shoulder and took the Colt in his left hand. The black crusader braced the stock of his assault rifle against his hip.

Both men scanned the roof, and the windows and rooftops of nearby buildings, in search of more hired killers. They found none. But at the far side of the roof, two bodies sprawled. The dead men wore dark blue police uniforms with SWAT shoulder patches. The cops had been shot several times in the back and at the base of the skull.

"Fuckin' bastards," Gross growled bitterly as he stared down at the dead police officers. "They crept up on the SWAT guys and murdered them in cold blood. They never had a chance to defend themselves."

"At least they died quickly," James commented. "And the creeps who did it to them ain't going anywhere but the morgue. By the way, that's where I'd be heading if you hadn't nailed that dude with the chopper. Thanks, man."

"Just part of the job," Gross said with a shrug.

James grinned. "Now let's—"

The rumble of an explosion drowned out his words. It came from the direction of Pier Fourteen. James and Gross watched with horror as the bait shop burst into flame.

"My God!" Gross gasped. "That was Leeper's stakeout. Three of your partners were there, too!"

THE MEN ON BOARD the garbage scow didn't unload any cocaine, but they did produce a LAW rocket launcher. The hoodlums aimed the weapon at the bait shop and fired the explosive antitank round into the shop. The eruption tore the building to pieces. Debris tumbled across the pier. The gunmen at the scow cheered and waved their weapons in a victory salute.

The gangsters were unaware that they had blown up an empty building.

The moment Yakov Katzenelenbogen had heard the shooting at the motel, he had ordered everyone to evacuate the bait shop immediately. Rafael Encizo and David McCarter had already gathered up their gear and had headed for the door, well aware of the danger. Lieutenant Leeper and Garfalo, realizing the Phoenix Force trio had been right about Polaski, had made no objection and had followed the others out the door.

"Son of a bitch," Leeper rasped as they crouched behind a warehouse. "Those bastards are serious!"

"So are we," Encizo remarked. The weapon he aimed at the garbage scow resembled an oversize flare pistol with an enormous muzzle.

He fired the H&K M-69. The compact grenade launcher lobbed a 40 mm projectile directly into the center of the garbage scow. The grenade exploded, blasting the flybridge and cabin. Two mutilated bodies were among the wreckage that showered the startled hoodlums at the pier. Flames burst from the engine at the bow of the boat. The deck began to burn, and columns of thick dark smoke rose from the damaged vessel.

"Miami Police!" Leeper shouted from the shelter of the warehouse. He peered at the surviving thugs across the sights of his CAR-15. "You're under arrest!"

The gunsels swung their weapons in the direction of Leeper's voice. The vice cop promptly triggered his carbine and pumped a trio of 5.56 mm rounds into the chest of the closest hood. The guy dropped his machine pistol and tumbled to the plank walk.

Katzenelenbogen stepped around the corner of the warehouse, the Uzi submachine gun braced across his prosthesis. The Israeli opened fire, spraying two more gunmen with 9 mm slugs. Their bloodied bodies convulsed from the impact and fell dying to the pier. Three surviving gunmen bolted for cover behind a stack of wooden crates.

Lieutenant Garfalo tried again to contact his SWAT team on the walkie-talkie. He cursed under his breath when he failed to get a response. When he looked up he saw two Hispanic gunmen with their sawed-off shotguns aimed at him.

He grabbed for his CAR, although he realized he couldn't reach the carbine in time. Suddenly, one of the gunsels fell forward, a crimson blob staining his shirtfront. The bullet that caught him in the back of the head smashed a gory exit wound in the center of his face.

Gary Manning shifted the aim of his FAL assault rifle to train the weapon on the second shotgun man. The hoodlum turned sharply and fired his twelve-gauge blaster. Buckshot pellets sparked concrete less than a yard from Manning's feet. The Canadian was out of range of the cut-down shotgun.

The FAL, however, had considerably greater distance. Manning squeezed the trigger twice, firing two 7.62 mm slugs into his opponent's chest. The shotgunner started to fall backward. Garfalo had seized his CAR-15 and triggered a full-auto salvo into the already dying man's torso. The multiple 5.56 mm bullets spun the guy's body around. Leaking blood like red wine through a strainer, the man collapsed to the ground.

"*¡Cristo!*" Carlos Benitez cursed softly as he watched the gun battle through the windshield of the old Chevy parked across the street from the pier.

The Cuban gangster and his driver climbed from the car and raced to a slate-gray minivan. Benitez hammered a fist on the doors at the rear of the van. The *marielitos* in the back of the vehicle responded immediately, scrambling from the van carrying an M-60 machine gun. Benitez didn't have to tell the Cuban-born gunmen what to do. They quickly set up the machine gun, aiming it at Pier Fourteen.

Twin beams of headlights suddenly flashed across the *marielitos*. The hoodlums stared at the flower delivery van that hurtled toward them. Detective Carlos Phillips drove the van. His partner, Ron Johnson, leaned out the passenger window, firing a stainless-steel Colt Commander at the *marielitos*. His aim was perfect, despite the motion of the moving vehicle.

Two .45 caliber slugs slammed into the torso of the Cuban thug behind the M-60. He screamed and tumbled to the pavement. Another *marielito* grabbed the M-60 and tried to swing its barrel toward the charging van. Benitez and another thug drew pistols from shoulder leather and fired at the vice cops.

Phillips ducked low behind the steering wheel as a 9 mm slug punched through the windshield and plowed into the backrest beside him. The mulatto cop sucked air through clenched teeth and stomped the gas pedal. Johnson fired two more rounds at the *marielitos* and retreated inside the window. One of his .45 slugs struck Benitez in the right shoulder, shattering the joint. Benitez cried out and dropped his H&K autoloader.

Benitez and one of his hoods dashed from the path of the charging flower van. The other two remained with the M-60, hoping to use it against the attacking vehicle. Their time ran out when Phillips rammed the pair with the van.

The broken body of one was propelled eight feet by the impact. The other *marielito* was knocked flat by the vehicle, his chest crushed under a rolling tire. Benitez and the other survivor ran toward the pier as another *marielito* gunman emerged from the front seat of the minivan, an Ingram M-11 in his fists.

The gunman with Benitez fired his Beretta 9 mm pistol at the flower van as he ran. The bullet punched into the metal skin of the vehicle, inches from Detective Johnson's head as the vice cop opened the door and returned fire. He nailed the triggerman with two .45 rounds. The guy fell to the pavement. Benitez kept running.

Detective Phillips stomped the brake, shifted gears to park and kicked open the door at the driver's side. He jumped from the vehicle with a cut-down double-barrel shotgun in his fists. The *marielito* who approached from the minivan aimed his Ingram at Johnson. Phillips's shotgun roared. Double O buckshot smashed the gunman's chest into pulp and slammed his corpse to the ground.

The hoodlums at the pier fired their weapons from the cover of the crates. David McCarter took an SAS flash-bang grenade from his belt, pulled the pin and hurled the blaster at the crates. The concussion grenade exploded, bowling over the heavy wooden boxes.

The crates crashed into the hoodlums, knocking two of them into the water. The third man staggered across the plank walk, stunned by the explosion, but he still held his machine pistol. David McCarter stepped forward and aimed his M-10 Ingram at the dazed hood.

"Drop it or kiss your ass goodbye," the Briton barked.

The gunman blinked with surprise and started to raise his weapon. McCarter fired his M-10 and stitched a trio of 9 mm bullet holes in the hoodlum's chest, tearing him open from throat to solar plexus. The goon fell backward and toppled into the bay.

Encizo and Garfalo joined McCarter. They moved to the edge of the pier to cover the two hoods still splashing around in the water. Seeing the weapons aimed at them, they cried out that they surrendered. Encizo instructed them in Spanish to swim to the pier and climb out of the water.

His right arm dangling from his bullet-crushed shoulder, Carlos Benitez staggered toward the warehouse. Blood drenched his jacket sleeve. The Cuban hood gasped and panted with exhaustion. He fell to one knee and clutched his wounded shoulder with his left hand.

"Didn't you hear the lieutenant?" Katz inquired as he pointed his Uzi at Benitez's face. "You're under arrest."

"*Sí, señor...*" the Cuban replied feebly. Then his eyes rolled up into his head, and he fainted.

8

Leonardo Scaletta didn't resist when the Miami police stopped him as he stepped from an expensive Italian restaurant in the Coconut Grove area. They flashed their shields and informed Scaletta that a Lieutenant Leeper, in Vice, wanted to talk to him.

"Am I under arrest?" the middle-aged, stocky Italian-American inquired with a confident smile. "It's been a long time since I saw a cop show on TV. Better read me my rights."

"You're not under arrest unless you refuse to come with us," Detective Johnson explained.

"It'll be better for you if you just come along, Mr. Scaletta," Detective Phillips added.

"Just wanna ask some questions, huh?" Scaletta turned to his two burly bodyguards and said, "You guys head home and tell Augie I'll be at the police station for a while. Tell him to have my lawyers on call in case I need 'em. And those bums damn well better drop everything else if that happens. They haven't been earning their keep lately."

"Right, Mr. Scaletta," the goon, who had mastered a certain degree of human speech, replied. His partner just grunted.

"Oh," Scaletta added, "tell my wife not to worry. I should be home for supper."

"Maybe," Johnson muttered. "Come on, hotshot."

Fifteen minutes later, Scaletta sank into a chair in Lieutenant Leeper's office. Yakov Katzenelenbogen and Harold Krebs were also present. Scaletta removed a leather cigar case from his jacket pocket and smiled at Leeper.

"Haven't I met you before?" he inquired. "About six months ago? Brought me in for questioning about cocaine or somethin' like that. But you dropped charges."

"This time we're talking about conspiracy to commit murder," Leeper replied grimly. "Six police officers were killed last night at a stakeout. One of them was a crooked cop, the other five were members of a SWAT team. They were shot in the back by *marielito* gunmen."

"What's that?" Scaletta asked with mock curiosity. "Some sort of Cuban street gang, isn't it?"

"They're a lot more than that and you know it," Leeper told him. "This particular bunch of *marielitos* was led by a fellow named Carlos Benitez. We caught Benitez alive, and he's singing like a canary. Guess whose name came up?"

"Some cheap spic hood claims I'm connected with gunning down police officers and you believe him?" Scaletta chuckled. "I think I'll call my lawyers now."

"Before you do that," Krebs began, "you'd better know that a DEA agent called Paris was also arrested last night. Turns out he was working for a criminal outfit called MERGE. Apparently it's a combination of the Mafia, the Colombian syndicate and some other organizations. He tells us the Scaletta Family is involved with MERGE, and he was getting his payoffs directly from Dominick Leone, your capo."

"The *marielitos* under Benitez have been working as a death squad for MERGE," Katz added, leaning forward to stare directly into Scaletta's face. "We've got some little fish, nasty killer fish, but little nonetheless. We want the big fish behind this open season on police and federal agents. So far, you're the biggest fish we've got."

"You don't have me, fella." Scaletta laughed. "If you did, I'd be under arrest."

"I can arrest you right now," Leeper said with a shrug. "It'd be a pleasure to arrest you. Of course, you'd be out on bail before sunset, and you'd go home and start pulling strings with judges and politicians, buying off witnesses. It's fifty-fifty you'd go to trial and walk out a free man."

"It's happened before," Scaletta replied.

"But this time," Katz declared, "someone will kill you."

"What the fuck?" Scaletta glared at him. "Is that a threat? Who the hell are you, anyway?"

"No one in this room knows my real name," Katz said with a smile. "And I'm not making a threat. I'm simply saying someone would kill you. Pick you off with a sniper rifle at four hundred meters. Blow you up in your Mercedes with a grenade launcher. Garrote you in a public rest room. Take out the guards at your home with silenced weapons and kill you in your own bedroom. It will most certainly happen if there is no other way to touch you."

"What is this shit?" Scaletta demanded. "I wanna call my lawyers, damn it."

"Good idea," Katz agreed. "Make sure your will is in order."

"I used to play a lot of poker," Scaletta stated, looking at Katz. "I'm pretty good at guessing when a man's bluffing. I don't think you are."

"I've lost count of the number of men I've killed over the years," Katz said with steel in his voice. "Most were in self-defense. All were justified, in my opinion. But, I'm not saying I'd kill you. I simply said *someone* would."

"You're a real hardass, fella," Scaletta declared. "Okay. You guys didn't arrest me, so that means you wanna make a deal. Let's hear it."

"Paris and the *marielitos* tell us that you're basically a go-between for the Colombians and Bolivians in MERGE," Krebs stated. "They're bringing the cocaine into the country. They're financing the hits. All you've been doing is passing on orders and distributing coke to dealers in the rich neighborhoods. You're dirty, but the bastards behind you are even worse.''

"I can tell you where to find the guys you want here in the U.S.," Scaletta said quietly. "Here in Miami. And some of the MERGE kingpins in Texas, California and at least one in Chicago. But if you want Mr. Cocaine and Murder, you'll have to look for him south of the border."

"Colombia?" Katz inquired.

"Unless he's moved," Scaletta confirmed. "Calls himself El Tiburón—the Shark. He earned that title. He's the biggest, meanest fish in the coke trade. Too bad you can't touch him."

"Why not?" Katz asked.

"Hardass wants to know 'why not,'" Scaletta said, chuckling. "Figure you can just head down to Colombia and look up El Tiburón in the Bogotá phone book? Then you find him and just blow him away? Bullshit. Number one, you'll never find him. Number two, it won't do any good if you do."

"I hate to sound like a parrot who has memorized only one expression," Katz said, sighing, "but why not?"

"You ain't gonna find him because he's got politicians, cops, government agents, Christ knows what else on his payroll," Scaletta explained. "If you guys tried to find him, you'd get arrested, thrown in jail and murdered in your cell—if a flunky in uniform didn't shoot you for 'resisting arrest.'"

"Let's say we manage to get past those problems," Katz said, sticking to his point. "We find out where El Tiburón is. You still don't think we can get him?"

"Look, hardass," Scaletta said, chewing on his unlit cigar. "I haven't been down there, so I don't know, but a Colombian associate of mine tells me El Tiburón lives in a fortress somewhere in the jungle. The place is surrounded by a hostile tribe of Indians. Supposed to be headhunters or cannibals or somethin'. Anyway, they kill anybody who gets in the area. Even the Colombian army is scared of 'em. Somehow, El Tiburón managed to get on their good side. They'll protect his ass. Even if you made it past the Indians, the fortress is guarded by a fuckin' army of professional killers."

"I see," Katz said thoughtfully. "El Tiburón presents quite a challenge."

"You wanna find out how tough you really are?" Scaletta smiled. "Go to Colombia. You'll find out."

Katz smiled and nodded but said nothing.

"You ready to play ball with us, Scaletta?" Leeper asked. "Mr. Krebs and I can see to your protection as a federal witness. You will, of course, be free of prosecution."

"I can do it," Scaletta confirmed. "And you'll be able to shut down the hit teams here in the States…for a little while. But when El Tiburón learns what's happened, he'll set up the operation with new personnel, and it'll be business as usual by next month."

"Then we'll have to take care of El Tiburón," Katz stated as he headed for the door.

"You plan to go to Colombia, hardass?" Scaletta called to the Israeli. "Then you'd better make sure you've got *your* will in order."

"Thanks for the advice," Katz replied as he stepped from Leeper's office into the corridor.

KATZ MET WITH the other four members of Phoenix Force at Bayfront Park. The park was quiet and pretty, and offered splendid views of the pleasure craft that sailed in the bay. The commandos sat at a picnic table under a palm tree, eating sandwiches and drinking coffee and soft drinks. Several senior citizens were sunning themselves nearby, and an old Asian man was leading a class of younger students in t'ai chi exercises. The elderly teacher's slow, graceful movements showed muscle control that put his younger students to shame.

"So that's what I learned from Scaletta," Katz said, concluding his account of the meeting at Leeper's office. "What do you gentlemen think about the mission so far?"

"I think we'd have to be nuts to go to Colombia," Gary Manning replied.

"Right," David McCarter agreed. "So when do we leave?"

"Wait a minute," Calvin James urged, waving the chili dog in his hand. "Are we gonna tell Brognola about this? The dude can probably get us some friendly contacts down there.''

"It was hard enough to find anybody in the DEA or the Miami Police Department we could trust,'' Manning stated. "Colombia will be even worse. The cocaine syndicates practically run the country.''

"That's an exaggeration,'' Rafael Encizo replied. "The drug czars have a lot of influence, but they don't own the Colombian government. In 1984 the Colombian authorities raided a huge cocaine refinery about four hundred miles from Bogotá. The syndicate had set up quite a complex. There were nineteen laboratories for processing cocaine, and barracks that accommodated eighty people. The Colombian cops arrested forty coke workers and confiscated fourteen tons of cocaine.''

"Fourteen tons?'' Manning wondered if he had heard incorrectly.

"That's right,'' Encizo confirmed. "Up until the raid, the Colombian government estimated about fifty tons of cocaine were processed in their country every year. But that one complex was producing six times that much.''

"Christ!'' Manning said, shaking his head. "The more we learn about the cocaine business, the worse the problem becomes. It's so big, so powerful, I don't see how we can even put a dent in it.''

"Dealing with the cocaine traffic itself isn't our mission,'' Katz reminded him. "The organized murder of police and federal officers is what we have to stop. But if we take out El Tiburón, we'll accomplish our mission *and* put more than a dent in the drug trade.''

"Good," McCarter said with a nod. He took a pack of Player's from his pocket and shook out a cigarette. "So let's head for Colombia and find this Shark, and make fish sticks out of him."

"Have you been listening, David?" Manning asked, staring at the Briton as if he thought McCarter might need a lobotomy. "If we go to Colombia we won't have any backup, we won't have any contacts with a friendly government or even a guide to help us find our way around down there."

"Yeah," James agreed. "Even when we went into Czechoslovakia, we had help from the anticommunist resistance."

"Well, David?" Manning said. "Let's hear about your old chum in Colombia."

"What old chum in Colombia?" the Briton replied.

"In England you had a gunrunner who helped us," the Canadian answered. "In Hong Kong you knew a crook involved in vice. I'm still trying to figure out what that guy did in the Philippines. Anyway, you've got dozens of friends, of questionable morals and habits, scattered all over the world. So don't you know a forger or a smuggler living in Bogotá?"

"Sorry to disappoint you, mate," McCarter said dryly, "but I don't know anybody in Colombia."

James turned to Encizo. "Rafael, you've spent a lot of time in Central and South America. You got any contacts in Colombia?"

"None that I know of," the Cuban answered "Maybe there's a DEA agent stationed there who I once worked with, or maybe one of my old comrades-in-arms from the Bay of Pigs lives in Colombia now. But I doubt it."

Katz drained his Styrofoam coffee cup, and grimaced at a mouthful of grounds. "If we go to Colombia to hunt down El Tiburón, we'll have to do it alone. No contacts. No backup."

"And we'll have to go in virtually naked," Manning added.

"Come on," McCarter drawled, "they won't let us on the bleedin' plane if we don't have any clothes on."

"I'm talking about weapons and you know it," the Canadian retorted. "We can't smuggle in much weaponry in the false bottom of a suitcase."

"Well," James said with a sigh, "I sure hope we can come up with a real good plan. We're gonna need it."

9

The 747 landed at the international airport in Bogotá. A tall black man and a muscular Hispanic presented passports that claimed they were Archibald Wells and Tomás Rivera. While customs inspectors examined their hand luggage almost casually, a bored-looking man in a blue uniform and carrying a clipboard checked their passports, nodded, then handed them back to the visitors.

"Norteamericanos," he commented disdainfully, as if their nationality was a dread disease. *"No habla inglés..."*

"We both speak Spanish, *señor*," Rafael Encizo assured him.

"Bueno," the inspector replied. "You in Colombia for business or pleasure?"

"A little of both," James answered with a smile. He had learned Spanish as a kid in Chicago, and used some expressions peculiar to Puerto Ricans and Mexicans that were uncommon in Europe or South America. His accent wavered from Sonora to San Juan, with a trace of south-side Chicago slipping in.

"I see," the inspector said dryly. He already suspected that Wells and Rivera were more than mere tourists. "Make certain your business is legal. And let me warn you, our inspection of luggage leaving Colombia is somewhat more thorough than when one enters the country. Especially for visitors from *los Estados Unidos*."

"We'll bear that in mind, *señor*," Encizo assured him.

"Enjoy your stay in Colombia," the inspector said without sincerity.

In the baggage delivery area, Encizo and James found there were no conveyor belts as in most modern airports. A porter pushed in a cart loaded with suitcases. There, as everywhere in the airport, soldiers armed with submachine guns were on patrol. They stared at James and Encizo, eyes filled with suspicion. The Phoenix Force pair, along with a handful of other Americans, claimed their luggage.

Three Colombians caught James's eye, and he nudged Encizo and nodded toward the trio. They wore silk suits and expensive-looking rings and wristwatches. Bulges under their armpits suggested they were packing weapons. The porter approached them and gave a brown valise to the guy in the middle. The dude looked at it and shook his head. Then one of his companions handed the porter an apparently identical brown valise.

"I think we just witnessed a dope deal," James muttered. He glanced at the soldiers. "Those guys didn't even seem to notice."

"The soldiers are watching for the same thing every armed guard in an airport is watching for these days," Encizo replied. "Terrorism, not drugs, is a major problem here. Remember when a gang of extremists seized control of the Dominican embassy in Bogotá? The situation got so bad, President Betancur agreed to sign a truce with the three major left-wing guerrilla outfits, hoping to end the violence."

"That didn't work out too well," James commented.

"Negotiating with terrorists seldom works," Encizo agreed. "Neither does negotiating with gangsters. Let's get out of here."

They rented a Volkswagen Rabbit, and Encizo drove while James consulted a street map. The traffic was light as they pulled onto the Simón Bolívar Highway. One of the major roads in South America, the Simón Bolívar Highway crossed Colombia and extended to the capital cities of Venezuela and Ecuador. Unlike many roads in Colombia, it was in good condition.

Battered old trucks and army jeeps traveled the highway. An occasional rider on a bicycle or moped wheeled along the edge of the road. Encizo turned onto Córdoba Boulevard and headed for the heart of Bogotá, in search of the Hotel de Colombia. The main streets of the city were pitted with ruts and potholes.

Peasants with carts and pack animals, even chickens, shared the streets with motor vehicles.

Most of the buildings were simple wood or adobe structures. Street merchants hawked beads and pottery, offering "valuable Indian relics" for "a ridiculously low price." Children in tattered clothing chased after the cars.

"Well, Calvin," Encizo said with a grin as he steered the Rabbit around a beer truck parked in front of a restaurant, "how do you like Colombia so far?"

"I think I'd rather be back in Miami," James replied. "I hope that smuggler's tip doesn't turn out to be a bum steer."

James referred to information they had acquired from one of the smugglers in Miami, who had been interrogated after the incident at Pier Fourteen. The guy was a Colombian who claimed to take orders directly from Juan Rameriz Cordova, who he said was a lieutenant of El Tiburón. In fact, Cordova was said to be the Shark's top man in Bogotá.

"We questioned him under scopolamine," Encizo remarked. "You injected the truth serum. Figure he could lie under the influence?"

"I doubt it," James replied. "I'm just not sure he had his facts straight. If Cordova is as high up in the syndicate as our little canary claimed, he wouldn't tell a flunky any more than he absolutely had to."

"What are you worried about?" Encizo asked. "Our squealer didn't know anything about Cordova except his name and where he *might* be found. That's not a hell of a lot.''

''You sure know how to comfort a guy,'' James muttered as they approached their hotel.

Reservations for Mr. Rivera and Mr. Wells had been made in advance. Their room was drab, with faded wallpaper, cobwebs in the corners and a minimum of crudely made furniture. Roaches scurried for cracks in the wall when Encizo flicked on the single light bulb that hung from the ceiling.

''Reminds me of my old neighborhood,'' James commented with disgust.

''Hopefully, we won't have to spend too much time here,'' Encizo replied. ''Let's get unpacked and find a stiff drink or two.''

They didn't discuss their mission in the room. Though it was unlikely the Shark's syndicate had planted listening devices there, it was possible. Phoenix Force couldn't afford to underestimate a criminal organization financed by billions of dollars. El Tiburón could afford to hire well-trained intelligence personnel and experts in industrial espionage. Two men from the United States, taking a hasty trip to Colombia, making reservations at the first available hotel only hours before they arrived, might arouse suspicion in a spy of El Tiburón planted in the national telephone company.

What was more likely was that the Colombian government might have the room bugged. The American visitors could be under surveillance if the government suspected them of being drug smugglers, trying to make a deal with the syndicate. Either the government or the syndicate could ruin the mission. The Phoenix pair had to be careful to avoid detection.

The two men quickly unpacked their clothes and other belongings from the suitcases. Then each took a plastic credit card from his wallet. The VISA cards were special issues in the cover names of Wells and Rivera. Each snapped a narrow plastic strip off the bottom of his card, and slid the strip into a slot hidden under the lining of his suitcase.

The strips from the cards were actually plastic "flat keys." The embossed expiry dates activated computer-programmed tumbler locks to the secret compartments inside the cases. The false bottom of each suitcase was lined with lead to avoid detection by X rays at customs. Phoenix Force had used the false bottoms before to smuggle small objects past airport security.

The "small objects" they had smuggled into Colombia were two Sterling Model 302 automatics, two Gerber bolt-action folding knives, two pairs of infrared goggles and two compact bug sweepers.

The Sterling pistols weighed only about thirteen ounces each and measured less than five inches in length. Yet a Sterling could carry six .22 Long Rifle cartridges. James and Encizo had two magazines for each weapon.

The Gerber knife was basically a lock-blade folding knife, with a bolt-action release catch high on the

handle. It too was lightweight, with a three-inch, ra-
zor-sharp blade. Because the blade pivoted on a brass
bushing and locked in place, the knife could easily be
opened with one hand.

Both Encizo and James were experienced knife
fighters who had learned the deadly skill at a young
age. Neither man had much faith in switchblade
knives, which were often of poor quality, preferring a
good sheath knife or a quality lock-blade to a weapon
that might malfunction due to a cheap spring.

They loaded the pistols. Encizo tucked his Sterling
under his belt at the small of his back, then put on his
jacket to conceal it. James followed his example. They
pocketed the knives and spare magazines, but left the
infrared goggles and bug detectors sealed in the suitcase compartments. The spy gadgets would arouse
suspicion if found on them by someone searching
them.

As they left the room and Encizo locked the door,
James glanced up and down the corridor and hummed
a tune from an 007 film.

"Pity we couldn't use the Aston Martin for this
mission," he commented with a perfect Cambridge
accent. "But the bloody ejector seat wasn't ready for
the field. Bouncing up and down, up and down. Can't
have our villains hopping about like a bloody jack-in-
the-box...."

"Now that you mention it," Encizo replied, "I
think we should take a cab anyway. Probably take the
driver less time to find Los Extasiar."

"Yeah," James said sourly. "I can hardly wait to visit a bunch of killer gangsters, probably armed to the teeth, while all we've got are a couple of .22s and a pair of knives."

"Well, it could be interesting," Encizo replied with a shrug.

The pair took a cab to Los Extasiar. The driver took the scenic route, naming the sights as he drove past the National Library and Plaza Bolívar. He had noticed that both men spoke Spanish with an accent that wasn't Colombian. Figuring they were unfamiliar with the city, he took a roundabout drive to run up his meter.

James and Encizo suspected what he was up to but didn't complain. They were in no rush to find Los Extasiar, and the cabbie's tour was an easy way for them to learn more about the city.

The cabdriver cruised by the Gold Museum and suggested his passengers might want to see the displays of pre-Columbian art, then he finally headed for their destination in east Bogotá.

Los Extasiar was a sleazy-looking nightclub on Palmira Street. Its thick, frosted windows were spotted with filth. Next to its winking neon sign was a poster of a well-endowed woman with long black hair. She wore a skimpy costume and a mask with pointed cat ears.

Encizo and James pushed through the thick curtains at the entrance. The interior of Los Extasiar was dimly lit by small red and blue bulbs. A Spanish ballad played too loudly over stereo speakers. On a center stage, two naked women gyrated to the drumbeat that dominated the music while strobe lights played on their bodies.

Business was slow in the club at three in the afternoon. All the patrons were male, but only a few seated at tables were watching the nude dancers. The others were clustered at a long leather-topped bar. They spoke softly, often to the heavyset man behind the counter. James and Encizo approached him.

"Buenas tardes," the bartender greeted them. "What would you like to drink?"

"We wish to speak with Señor Cordova," Encizo replied, placing a fifty-dollar bill on the bar. "Privately. *¿Comprende?"*

"Señor Cordova is not expecting any visitors," the bartender said with a shrug. "He does not like to be disturbed without very good reason."

"We have some good reasons," James assured him. "About two million of them."

"Where are you gentlemen from?" the bartender asked.

"Where we're from doesn't matter," Encizo replied, placing another fifty-dollar bill on the counter. "But we represent a group of clients in Europe. Wealthy clients, who wish to do business with Señor Cordova and El Tiburón."

"Sharks can be very dangerous," the bartender stated.

"Many things are dangerous," Encizo answered. "But one risks certain dangers when the profit is great."

"Un momento, por favor," the barman urged. He moved to the end of the counter and spoke to a big, muscular man who looked like a bouncer.

The bartender returned to James and Encizo. "That gentleman I just spoke to will take you to Señor Cordova."

"Gracias, señor," Encizo said, placing one more fifty-dollar bill on the bar.

The bouncer silently escorted the pair to a door at the rear of the building. He knocked twice, waited, then rapped his knuckles on the panel once more. The door opened a crack, and a man's eye peered through the gap.

"Espera," the bouncer told Encizo and James in a voice that sounded like sandpaper rasping against hardwood. "Wait."

The bouncer was allowed into the room, and the door closed behind him. A few seconds later it opened again, and a bean-pole-thin man with a face like a copper mask stared at James and Encizo with reptilian eyes. He jerked his head sideways, signaling them to enter.

Encizo and James stepped into an office with a plush carpet, brown leather chairs and a walnut bookcase and desk. Behind the desk was a man in his mid-thirties. His black hair was thinning at the top, and a knife scar marred the left cheek of his angular face.

"I am Juan Cordova," he announced in a flat voice. "You will both face the wall, spread your arms and legs and place your hands on the wall."

"Do it now," the tall man with the rigid features instructed, pointing a 9 mm Largo pistol at the pair.

The muscle-bound bouncer also aimed a pistol at the two Phoenix Force warriors. James and Encizo raised their hands to shoulder level and turned to the wall, standing spread-eagle while Cordova's men frisked them with professional thoroughness.

The hoodlums immediately found and confiscated the .22 pistols and Gerber folding knives. Then they checked for ankle holsters and sleeve knives and tore open shirt buttons to search for hidden microphones. At last the hoods stepped away from James and Encizo and placed the confiscated weapons, passports and wallets on Cordova's desk.

"Rivera and Wells," Cordova remarked, inspecting the passports. "You're from *los Estados Unidos*. I have been there many times. Miami, Los Angeles, New York City. I like your country. They have much money in the United States."

He examined the Sterling pistols and chuckled. "You *norteamericanos* like guns, but I don't see any permits for you to carry *pistoles* in my country. Maybe I should have you arrested."

"You friendly with the police?" James inquired, still standing spread-eagle. He glanced over his shoulder at Cordova. "That's not what we heard."

"Shut up, Wells," Encizo hissed in English. He switched back to Spanish and addressed Cordova. "We came to make a deal with you and you're talking about sending us to jail."

"I'm sure you could call the United States embassy and they'd take care of you," Cordova answered. "You might be deported back to the United States, but I doubt that you'd be in any serious trouble."

"You think we're DEA agents?" James inquired. He uttered a slight laugh. "Hear that, Rivera? Imagine us being mistaken for cops!"

"It won't be so funny if they turn us over to the authorities," Encizo replied. "Señor Cordova, my partner and I have criminal records in the United States. We'll be in considerable trouble if we get deported back there for carrying unlicensed firearms here in Colombia. If you don't want to deal with us, we'll pay you one thousand dollars just to forget you ever met us. We'll make our deal someplace else.... But you're turning down an excellent opportunity to make a large profit."

"Really?" Cordova smiled. "Tell me about it."

"Are you familiar with the Union de Corse?" Encizo asked. "The Corsican syndicate of Western Europe?"

"They're gangsters who deal in heroin," Cordova replied with a shrug. "They used to supply heroin to the Mafia in the United States. I believe they called this the French Connection. Why should these European hoodlums interest me?''

"Cocaine is becoming increasingly popular in Europe," Encizo explained. "A family in the Corsican syndicate wants to get into the coke business. Wells and I are just middlemen for the Corsicans."

"How are you suppose to work this deal?" Cordova asked. "A large shipment of cocaine would be worth millions of pesos. A very large shipment would be worth millions of American dollars. The Corsicans wouldn't trust that much money to a couple of small-time criminals like you two."

"We were sent to make the contacts with El Tiburón," Encizo stated. "The Corsicans are sending their own people to set up the rest of the deal. They'll handle the payment."

"That's an interesting story," Cordova said. "When are the Corsicans supposed to arrive?"

"They should be here the day after tomorrow," Encizo told him. "They're arriving on Air France flight 389, from Paris to Bogotá."

"Very interesting," Cordova repeated. He gestured to his men. "Return their passports, wallets and weapons."

"Does this mean we have a deal?" Encizo asked as the henchmen handed him his belongings.

"It means you're getting back your weapons and ID," Cordova answered simply. "For now, that's all it means. Hector will inform my bartender to give you gentlemen anything you want to drink...on the house.''

The muscle-bound flunky grunted and nodded.

"You're welcome to stay at Los Extasiar and enjoy the ladies and drink the fine spirits here," Cordova told them. "By the way, the dancers aren't whores, but if you want to spend some time with one of them, let Hector know. He'll make sure the lady obliges you."

The bouncer cracked his knuckles and smiled.

"However," Cordova added, "the women aren't on the house, and they're rather expensive."

"Señor Cordova is telling you this meeting is over," the skinny henchman with the hard face declared.

"I'm sure they understand that, Luis," Cordova said. "I've enjoyed this conversation, gentlemen. Perhaps we'll talk again."

10

"You think Cordova will go for it?" Calvin James asked Rafael Encizo as the pair ate supper in a small restaurant across the street from the Hotel de Colombia.

"He'll have to contact El Tiburón first," the Cuban answered. "Cordova isn't high enough up on the syndicate ladder to make a big deal with a European supplier. He'll also try to find out if we're telling the truth. Cordova thinks we might be DEA, but I doubt that he's very suspicious of that."

"The bastard keeps a good poker face," James commented. "Hard to say what was going through his head. But he must believe we're not cops or he would have called the police to arrest us for packing heat without a permit. That would have thrown a monkey wrench in any scheme the DEA might have had to use our contact with Cordova as a means of getting info on El Tiburón. It sure as hell would have loused up *our* plan if he'd called the cops."

"A man like Cordova doesn't want anything to do with the police," Encizo commented, sipping rich black Colombian coffee. "Besides, if the DEA or the Colombian government wanted to infiltrate the syndicate, they wouldn't use Americans, they'd send Colombian operatives. The CIA might have sent a cutout, but they'd probably insist he meet Cordova without carrying a weapon, because that can attract attention."

"Yeah," James agreed. "But dope dealers and smugglers carry weapons. It would have seemed a lot more suspicious if we'd been unarmed. How do you think El Tiburón will react when Cordova tells him about us?"

"The Shark probably has moles inside the Colombian government," Encizo answered. "Including the Justice Department, which works with the American DEA. He'll try to find out if we're government or DEA. Of course, we've already got Cordova's flunkies following us."

"I noticed," James said dryly.

He glanced at the small, mousy-looking man seated at a table across the room. The guy was pretending to read a newspaper. A person might move his head from side to side while scanning a newspaper, but he wouldn't scan the same sheet for fifteen minutes. The man had followed them into the restaurant and had been surreptitiously observing them ever since.

"Well, if our room wasn't bugged before, it will be now," Encizo remarked. "We could sweep for bugs, but that would make them more suspicious. We'd better not go near a telephone for a while or they'll figure we're contacting Washington.''

"The less time we spend in that dreary room the better," James stated emphatically.

"Right," the Cuban replied, glancing at his wristwatch. "We've still got plenty of time to kill. We'd better do something that's in character with the image we're trying to present to Cordova."

"Oh, darn," James said with mock dismay. "Does that mean we've gotta go to some night spots and drink, party and carry on with members of the opposite sex?"

"This is an important mission, Calvin," Encizo replied with a straight face. "We have to be willing to make certain sacrifices."

JAMES AND ENCIZO WOKE to the hammering of a fist on the door of their hotel room. Both reached instinctively for the pistols hidden in shoes under their beds. Encizo looked at his watch. Seven o'clock, he noticed. James climbed from his bed and walked to the door, clad only in his briefs.

"Who is it?" he asked, deliberately slurring his words. He repeated the question in Spanish. *"¿Quién llama?"*

"El portero," a voice answered.

"What the fuck!" James growled. "There's no doorman in this dump. Who the hell are you?"

"Señor Cordova sent me," the voice stated. "Open the door."

James turned to Encizo. The Cuban held a Sterling .22 in his fist. He slid his hand and the gun under a pillow, then nodded to James. The black man opened the door.

Luis, the tall guy with the copper face and lifeless eyes, stood in the doorway. He was accompanied by two young toughs dressed in flashy, multicolored shirts and white chinos. The trio entered.

"You two have a good time last night?" Luis inquired.

"What I remember about it was pretty good," Encizo replied. He sat up in bed, a hand pressed against his forehead as if suffering from a hangover.

"I remember the girls we had up here," James said with a lewd chuckle. "They sure were something. Where do you go to pick up women, Luis?"

"I did not come here to discuss such matters," the tall henchman said, his tone flavored by disgust. "Señor Cordova wishes to see you. Be at Los Extasiar at noon."

The Phoenix Force pair followed instructions. At twelve o'clock precisely they arrived at the nightclub. Cordova was alone except for Luis, and Encizo and James weren't frisked. The Phoenix commandos realized Cordova had checked them out and decided they were telling the truth.

"You were right about Flight 389 from Paris," Cordova remarked as he sat behind his desk and fired up a foot-long Havana cigar. "It is due to arrive tomorrow morning."

"That's what we said," Encizo replied. "Now, how about the deal?"

"We'll handle that, Rivera," Cordova answered. "We'll need the names and descriptions of the Corsicans."

"What do you mean?" Encizo asked. "Wells and I are supposed to meet them at the airport."

"That plan has just been changed," Cordova said with a cruel smile. "Your role in this business is finished. Go back to *los Estados Unidos*. Your Corsican friends can arrange to pay you there."

"That's not how it works, Cordova," James told him. The black man started to rise from his chair.

"You two have been dismissed," Luis declared, pointing his Largo pistol at James's head. "Get out while you still can."

"Luis—" Cordova began in a hard voice.

"What is this crap?" Encizo demanded, jumping from his chair.

Luis swung his pistol toward the Cuban. James took advantage of the distraction. His left hand slapped the bottom of Luis's fist, knocking the Largo toward the ceiling. James's right hand clasped the thug's piece. He jammed a finger between the firing pin and hammer to prevent Luis from firing the weapon.

James then delivered a back kick, driving the back of his heel between Luis's legs. The hood moaned in breathless agony as James wrenched the pistol from his grasp. The black warrior applied a wrist lock with his right hand while holding the confiscated Largo in his left. He hauled Luis forward and tripped him with an extended leg.

Luis fell to the floor, his breath driven from his lungs. He stared into the muzzle of the Sterling Model 302 in Encizo's fist. The Cuban aimed the pistol at Luis's face and smiled as the hood spread his fingers to reveal empty palms.

"Don't push the button under your desk for your men to come in," Encizo told Cordova, although he was still watching Luis. "You don't need them."

"I'm glad to hear that," Cordova stated, holding his hands at shoulder level. "How did you know I have a button under my desk to signal help?"

"Because you're too smart not to have one," Encizo replied.

"We have to talk about this deal," James stated. He pressed the release catch of the Largo pistol and dumped the magazine on the floor. He worked the slide to pump the cartridge from the chamber, then tossed the empty gun onto a chair.

"All right," Cordova agreed with a smile. "Let's talk."

"Our deal with the Corsicans is to meet them at the airport," Encizo explained, putting his Sterling .22 in a jacket pocket. "We're supposed to be paid here in Colombia. Otherwise, the Corsicans might welch on the deal. We didn't come all this way to be cheated."

"And we know who the Corsicans are," James added. "We know what they look like and what names they're using."

"Señor Cordova," Luis said as he slowly got to his feet, "allow me to get Hector and a couple of the others. We shall make these scum talk."

"We've still got guns," Encizo declared. "If your men try to jump us, we'll fight back. You'll have to kill us."

"And we'll take a few of your men with us," James added. "The Corsicans are paying us. You've got nothing to lose by letting us stay with you. Besides, the Corsicans don't speak Spanish. You got anybody on your payroll who speaks French?"

"I might," Cordova replied with a shrug. "Do you speak French, Señor Wells?"

"Je lis, j'écris et je parle français," James replied.

"I'm impressed, Wells," Cordova admitted.

"I'm not," Luis hissed as he stepped toward James and swung a roundhouse punch at the black man's head.

James easily blocked the punch with his forearm and grabbed the hood's wrist. He turned quickly and pulled Luis's arm across his shoulder. James straightened his knees and bent at the waist. Luis cried out as he hurtled over James's shoulder and crashed to the floor. The guy's body bounced on impact. He moaned as he lay sprawled on the floor, holding one hand to his sore head.

"Very impressive, Señor Wells," Cordova said. "You speak at least three languages and you're trained in judo or karate or whatever you call it."

"I learned a few tricks when I was in the navy," James told him.

"You certainly aren't an ordinary racketeer errand boy." Cordova turned to Encizo. "Are you also full of surprises, Rivera?"

"We're not a couple of punk kids," Encizo answered. "The Corsicans figured we could handle the job, that's why they hired us. You think they'd trust a task like this to a couple of teenage junkies who'd snort up twenty thousand dollars' worth of coke before delivering it to the buyers? Or shoot off their mouths to the authorities?"

"A good point," Cordova agreed. "Very well. You two will go with us to the airport and meet these Corsicans. But you'll have to spend the night with us. I don't want you two out of my sight or the sight of my men until we've made the deal."

"What do you think, Wells?" Encizo asked James.

"Señor Cordova is willing to oblige us," James answered. "We should agree to his terms in return."

"All right," Encizo told Cordova. "We agree to your terms."

"Bueno," the hoodlum said, puffing his cigar. "Now, how much cocaine are we talking about?"

"Approximately twenty kilos," Encizo answered.

"That would be nearly sixteen million pesos," Cordova mused. "Close to two and a half million *norteamericano* dollars. What currency do they intend to pay us with?"

"Wells and I are to be paid in American currency," Encizo answered. "They didn't tell us what they want to pay you with. Probably dollars or Swiss francs."

"Either would be acceptable," Cordova said with a nod.

"So we just have to wait for tomorrow morning to get here," Encizo said with a smile.

"*¡Negruzco cochino!*" Luis spat at James as he started to rise from the floor.

"Your mama," the black man replied.

He stepped forward and slammed a hard uppercut to Luis's jaw. The punch knocked Luis unconscious to the floor. James sighed and turned to Cordova.

"You'd better not give us this *cabrón* for a room-mate," he remarked. "If he comes at me again, I'm going to kill him."

"I believe you," Cordova said, frowning. "Luis is supposed to be my chief enforcer, but I wonder if I should replace him. Perhaps we can do more business after this is finished."

"We'll talk about that possibility later," Encizo replied. "After this is over."

11

Flight 389 from France arrived at 8:35 the following morning. Juan Cordova, Calvin James and Rafael Encizo watched the passengers disembark. Yakov Katzenelenbogen, Gary Manning and David McCarter were among the people to descend from the plane.

The three Phoenix Force commandos had previously traveled to France, using forged American passports. Then they'd flown from Europe to Colombia, using forged French passports. It had been a long and tiresome journey, but it was all part of the charade to convince the Colombians that the three newcomers were members of the Corsican syndicate.

The trio wore tailored suits purchased in Paris and chatted with one another in fluent French. In case any of El Tiburón's men were able to eavesdrop on the conversation and understood French, Katz and Manning spoke with despair about the probability that they would not eat a decent meal until they returned to France. McCarter complained about the flight. He said he suspected the pilot was German, and he wondered why an American had been permitted to fly first-class in a French plane. Did the government care nothing for national security? What if Khaddafi had known of the American and put a bomb on the plane? The others agreed and shook their heads sadly. No one listening would have doubted the three were French citizens.

"Bonjour, Henri," Calvin James cried as the trio approached. *"Ah, vous voilà!"*

"Oui," Katz replied wearily. He stared at Cordova. *"Qui est celui-ci?"*

"C'est Monsieur Cordova," James answered. He turned to the Colombian and spoke in Spanish. "This is Henri Picard. That isn't his real name, of course, but that's what he's calling himself these days."

"Buenos días," Cordova said, extending his hand. "Welcome to Colombia."

Katz held his gloved right hand rigidly against his chest and took Cordova's hand with his left. The Israeli nodded and said, *"Buenos días, Monsieur Cordova."*

"We forgot to tell you that Picard has a crippled arm," Encizo told Cordova. "Some sort of bone cancer."

"Pity," Cordova said, but his tone revealed he felt nothing for the suffering of a stranger. "Do they want to take care of business immediately, or do they need to go to their hotel first?"

"I don't know," Encizo answered. "Wells speaks French. Not me. Did you hear the question, Wells?"

"Yes," James replied. "I'll ask Henri."

"Allons chercher nos bagages," Katz declared, holding some tags in his fist.

"They want to get their luggage," James explained.

"Very well," Cordova said with annoyance. "We can't really discuss business in the airport anyway."

He turned to Hector, the muscle-bound bouncer, and told him to escort the three Corsicans to the baggage room. Cordova instructed him to stay with the three and not allow them to open their suitcases. Instead, Cordova told his henchman to carry their luggage to the limousine outside.

"Excuse me, Señor Cordova," Encizo began; "but Picard may wish to go to the hotel and relax first. He may want to eat something and even contact his superiors in France."

"He can do any of those things," Cordova answered. "But he'll do them with us present. I don't want them out of our sight until the deal is complete. If Picard objects, he can go back to France and tell his customers to snort talcum powder up their nostrils."

"You want me to have Wells translate that?" Encizo asked.

"Go ahead," the Colombian replied. "These Corsicans might be powerful men in Europe, but they're on my turf now. They'll either agree to my terms or they can forget about doing business with us."

James spoke to Katz in French. The Israeli looked at Cordova and gave a helpless shrug. He turned to

McCarter and Manning and conversed briefly in whispered French. All three exchanged nods.

"So far, so good," James announced. "They're willing to accept your terms, Señor Cordova."

"Bueno," Cordova said with a nod. "We can get six people in my limo comfortably. Señor Picard and his two associates can join you and me, Wells. I'll need you to translate."

"I wish Luis wasn't driving," James muttered.

"Don't worry," Cordova assured him. "I'll keep Luis on a leash. Besides, he has more to fear from you than the other way around."

"I'm not worried about what he might do physically," James answered. "But I don't want him sounding hostile and making the Corsicans wonder what sort of outfit we've introduced them to. You might mention that to Luis. If he wants to settle a personal gripe with me, we'll see about it later. Right now, we've got a big deal to close."

"Good point," Cordova agreed. "I'll speak with Luis. Señor Rivera, you will join Hector and Manuel in the Jaguar."

"Sí, Señor Cordova," Encizo answered with a nod.

A short time later they met in the airport parking lot. The luggage was stored in the trunk of the limousine. With James as interpreter, Cordova requested one of Picard's men to ride up front with Luis. Katz asked Manning to do this. Cordova and James sat in the back, facing Katz and McCarter. The limo headed for the exit, followed by a black Jaguar, containing

Encizo, Hector and a young Colombian triggerman named Manuel.

"Ask Señor Picard if he had a pleasant trip," Cordova told James. The Colombian was unaware that McCarter's Spanish was fluent and that Katz and Manning knew the language well enough to get the gist of most of what was said.

"I don't think he's interested in social pleasantries," James commented, but he translated the question into French anyway.

Katz frowned and fired off a rapid sentence.

"He wants to know about the cocaine," James told Cordova. "He says he wants to make the deal today."

"Does he have the money with him?" Cordova asked.

James translated once more. Cordova noticed that Katz's response included the words "Panama" and "banque." He guessed the response before James explained.

"The money is in an account in a Panama bank," James stated. "Señor Picard says that you should be familiar with such transactions."

Banks in Panama had long been a favorite place for the *coquitos* to launder money. The cocaine czars could send cash to Panamanian bankers willing to keep their accounts confidential. The *coquitos* made additional profit from interest on their savings, and the bankers helped them invest in businesses and international stock and commodities.

"We've done business with banks in Panama before," Cordova confirmed. "But we haven't done business with Señor Picard before."

"Picard understood that El Tiburón had done business with Corsicans before," James stated. "Something about an outfit called MERGE?"

"*¡La Amalgamacíon!*" Cordova gasped, a trace of fear in his voice. "You did not tell me Picard was connected with MERGE. All business concerning MERGE is to be handled by El Tiburón himself."

"It seems the European branch of MERGE is concerned about some of El Tiburón's activities," James explained with a shrug. "Something to do with his actions in the United States. Do you know what that's all about?"

"I'm not at liberty to say," Cordova said nervously. It disturbed him that his boss might be in trouble with other forces in MERGE. That meant Cordova could also be in trouble.

"You contacted El Tiburón about the deal and he approved it, didn't he?" James asked. "So surely there's nothing to worry about."

"Of course." Cordova smiled. He didn't want to appear unnerved or lacking in confidence. "I'm certain the payment through the Panamanian banks will be no problem. Does Señor Picard wish to go to his hotel now or perhaps to a restaurant?"

James asked Katz the question in French, and the Israeli replied, smiling at Cordova and nodding.

"He wants to examine the cocaine," James told Cordova. "The man sitting next to Luis is Gaston Mathis, Picard's chemist. He wants Mathis to check the coke to make certain it's quality merchandise. Señor Picard apologizes for this, but he explains that it is required by his superiors."

"Immediately?" Cordova frowned.

"As soon as possible," James confirmed.

"*¡Cristo!*" the *coquito* cursed under his breath. "Luis?"

"*Sí, Señor Cordova,*" the driver replied. He glanced over his shoulder and narrowed his eyes when he saw James. "What do you wish?"

"Contact Hector on the radio," Cordova commanded. "Tell him to watch for any vehicles that might be following us. Then contact Captain Morales on the car phone. Tell him I want some privacy."

"Who is Morales?" James asked.

"A police captain with the Bogotá police precinct in the area of my club." Cordova smiled. "I get in touch with him whenever I want to be certain the local police won't interrupt any private transactions."

"Very convenient," James commented.

"Morales will arrange a distraction to keep the police busy," Cordova continued. "He might contact an arsonist to set fire to a building, or arrange for a truck to go out of control and crash into a store or school. Anything that will keep the police too busy to pay any attention to us. Once he even arranged for a sniper to shoot a couple of bystanders from a window. The gunman was one of Morales's police officers. I believe some drifter was arrested for the shooting."

"Clever," James commented, struggling to hide his loathing for Cordova and for the corrupt cops on his payroll. As a former police officer, James believed there was no lower scum on the face of the earth than a crooked cop.

As the limousine approached Los Extasiar, smoke could be seen billowing from a burning building about a block from Palmira Street. Obviously Captain Morales had followed orders and assigned an arsonist to provide a distraction. The members of Phoenix Force in the limo felt relief mingled with concern when they saw the smoke.

Their concern wasn't just for the lives and property of innocent Colombians endangered by the fire. They realized that Cordova hadn't needed to arrange such a drastic action just to prevent the police seeing his arrival at the nightclub with the three "Corsican visitors."

Cordova wanted privacy for another reason: he either planned to use violence or suspected it might be necessary. This was hardly good news for Phoenix Force.

The limousine and the Jaguar came to a halt behind Los Extasiar. The five men of Phoenix Force followed Juan Cordova to the rear door of the nightclub. The gangster's henchmen closely flanked the visitors. Hector and Manuel seemed neutral, as if this was just part of their job, but Luis continued to glare

at Calvin James. He obviously hoped the opportu
nity would arise for him to get even with the black
commando for beating him up the day before.

Cordova led them all through a short corridor to his
office. The Colombian whispered something to Hector and Manuel. They nodded in response and headed
for the public area of the nightclub. Cordova un-
locked his office door and invited the others to enter.

"What the hell is going on here, Cordova?" Rafael
Encizo demanded. "I thought we were going to make
a deal."

"That's right," the *coquito* agreed. "But according to my terms."

"Your terms are beginning to annoy us," James
told him. "Don't tell me you plan to make a major
cocaine sale here in your office. I thought you were too
smart for that."

"I'll overlook your lack of faith, gentlemen," Cor
dova replied. "Certain security precautions must be
observed, even with Corsican visitors who may or may
not belong to MERGE. Any failure on my part to take
adequate precautions would certainly leave a bad
impression on our guests."

Hector and Manuel appeared in the doorway and
pointed 9 mm Astra pistols at the supposed Corsicans. The pistols had sound suppressors attached to
threaded barrels. Katz, McCarter and Manning raised
their hands to shoulder level. McCarter rasped a Gal-
lic oath.

"Tell them not to be alarmed, Wells," Cordova urged. "We simply have to frisk them for weapons. Speaking of which, Wells and Rivera, surrender your pistols, *por favor*."

"If this is a double cross," Encizo commented, reluctantly handing his Sterling .22 to Hector, "it isn't a very smart one, Cordova."

"Don't worry," the Colombian assured him. "Unless your associates are not what they claim to be, no one will get hurt. Of course, if they're wearing a wire and work for Interpol, we're all going to be in a bad way."

"Your gun, *cabrón*," Luis spat as he jammed his pistol into James's kidney.

"Take it easy, hombre," the black warrior said, wincing with pain. He used the thumb and index finger of his left hand to remove the Sterling .22 from his pocket. Luis grabbed the diminutive pistol and shoved James aside.

Hector and Manuel expertly searched Katz, Manning and McCarter. The hoodlums were surprised to discover Katz's artificial forearm and hand. Hector apologized to the Israeli. Katz shrugged in reply.

"Excellent," Cordova announced a few moments later. "Our visitors aren't carrying weapons or hidden microphones." He turned to Calvin James. "Please explain that this was necessary. I'm sure they'll understand."

While James translated Cordova's explanation for the Corsicans, Cordova moved to the bookcase. He pressed a finger several times to the eye of a brass bookend shaped like a horse's head. Then he stepped back as the bookcase slid open on hinges to reveal a vault.

"The secret door can only be opened by pressing the button on the horse's head in the correct manner," Cordova stated proudly. "The code feeds a command to a small computer built into the panel. The age of technology has given us a new version of 'Open Sesame.' Impressive, isn't it?"

"What if someone tried to simply force the bookcase from the wall with a crowbar?" Encizo asked.

"He'd be blown to bits along with everything inside the secret vault," Cordova answered. "The computer not only unlocks the door, but also deactivates an explosive charge. If it isn't deactivated, the bomb will explode when the door is forced. Nothing in the vault would escape destruction."

The Colombian gestured to Luis and Manuel. They entered the vault and hauled out two burlap bags, each appearing to weigh more than twenty pounds. The men of Phoenix Force watched the henchmen carry the bags to Cordova's desk. They also noticed that Luis and Manuel had put their guns away. Hector still held his Astra autoloader, but the silenced pistol was pointed at the floor.

"Señor Wells," Cordova said, "ask Señor Picard to examine the merchandise, *por favor*."

Luis stepped away from the desk while Manuel opened the burlap sacks. Inside was white powder encased in clear polyethylene bags, each bag apparently weighing one kilo. Cordova gestured toward the cocaine and smiled.

"There it is, gentlemen," he announced. "Twenty kilos."

"Let's do it," Katz declared in English.

Juan Cordova understood English. His mouth fell open, and his eyes widened with surprise. Before he could shout a warning to his men, Rafael Encizo crashed into him. Both men fell to the floor. Encizo pinned Cordova and snapped open the blade of his Gerber bolt-action lock-blade. The hoods had forgotten to confiscate the knives when they relieved Encizo and James of their pistols.

"Shut your mouth or die," Encizo rasped, holding the blade at Cordova's throat.

Hector raised his silenced pistol, but Yakov Katzenelenbogen was quicker. He extended his right arm and pointed his index finger at the muscular hoodlum's face. The tip of the gloved finger spat flame. A .22 Magnum slug smashed into Hector's forehead. His eyes rolled upward. Hector dropped his weapon and tumbled lifeless to the floor.

Manuel hastily reached for the silenced Astra in his belt. David McCarter closed in rapidly and slashed a cross-body karate chop aimed at Manuel's throat. The Briton's hand missed its target and struck Manuel under the lower lip. The hood's head bounced from the blow, but he still managed to draw his weapon.

McCarter quickly seized Manuel's forearm and wrist. He slammed the thug's limb across a bent knee as if breaking a piece of wood for a camp fire. Bone cracked. Manuel cried out in pain, and his Astra fell from limp fingers.

The British ace rammed an elbow stroke to Manuel's breastbone. The hoodlum hit the floor with a breathless groan. McCarter leaped forward and landed on his opponent with both feet, delivering the vicious commando stomp with all his weight behind it. The Briton's heels crushed Manuel's sternum and drove shards of bone into the chest cavity. The Colombian thug convulsed in agony and vomited blood on McCarter's Italian shoes, then died.

Luis yanked his Largo pistol from shoulder leather, but Calvin James swung a crescent kick at the gunman's wrist. The Largo flew from Luis's grasp. The black man's left fist smacked into the hood's cheek as his right drew the Gerber folding knife from his pocket.

Luis swung an awkward kick toward James's groin. The Phoenix pro easily deflected the attack with the side of his left hand. Luis pulled the confiscated Sterling .22 from his jacket pocket but before he could snap off the safety catch, James rushed him. The black warrior flicked the blade of the Gerber open with his thumb and plunged it between the thug's ribs.

The force of James's charge drove both men into Cordova's desk. Luis opened his mouth to scream, but the Chicago hardass grabbed Luis's throat with his left hand. The Colombian desperately thumbed off the Sterling's safety catch. Strong hands suddenly seized his fingers and pulled hard, snapping bones like dry twigs. Manning had come to James's assistance and had broken Luis's hand to take the Sterling from his fractured fingers.

"Adíos, cabrón," James whispered as he drove the blade of his Gerber into Luis's solar plexus to pierce his heart.

McCarter scooped up Manuel's discarded Astra 9 mm pistol. Katz claimed Hector's weapon and searched the dead man to find the Sterling .22 taken from Encizo. The Israeli pocketed the diminutive gun and headed for the vault. Manning gathered up the Largo pistol that had belonged to Luis. He and McCarter stood guard with drawn pistols at the office door.

"Rafael?" Katz called from the vault. "Is that bastard Cordova still alive?"

"Yeah," Encizo replied. He still held his knife at Cordova's throat. "You want to talk to him?"

"Bring him in here," the Phoenix Force commander replied.

"Just a second," James urged as he used his knife to slice off the end of a lamp cord he had unplugged from the wall. "Let's put a bracelet on him first."

"On your belly," Encizo told Cordova, holding the Gerber point at the Colombian's ear as he forced him to roll over.

James bound Cordova's wrists together at the small of his back with the lamp cord. Encizo and James pulled the *coquito* to his feet and dragged him to the vault.

"You sons of bitches are dead," Cordova rasped vehemently as they pushed him into the secret room.

"Then this shouldn't hurt," Encizo growled. The Cuban slammed a fist into the Colombian's kidney. Cordova groaned in response. "Maybe ghosts can punch, eh, *chico*?"

"Jesus!" James whistled when he saw the weapons racks along the wall of the vault. "Nice arsenal."

Several automatic rifles, submachine guns and shotguns were mounted in the racks. A dozen military pistols were braced in another case, and two stubby weapons similar to American M-79 grenade launchers were propped in a corner. There were also cases of 9 mm, 7.62 mm and 11.25 mm ammunition.

"They seem to be Argentine military weapons," Katz remarked as he used his prosthesis to shove a 25-round magazine into the well of an FMK-3 submachine gun, similar in design to the Uzi he knew so well. "Everything's in mint condition."

"You're right," Encizo commented as he read the lettering on an ammo case. "It's from the Fábrica Militar de Armas Portátiles in Santa Fe. That's the main government arms factory for Argentina."

"Hey!" James said cheerfully, taking a Sistema Colt pistol from the rack. "This baby is an Argentine version of a 1911A-1 U.S. Government Colt. It's an 11.25 millimeter. That's the same as a .45 cal."

"I hope you two will be very happy together," Katz said dryly. He pointed at a metal box in a corner. "What's that, Cordova?"

"Why don't you see for yourself?" the Colombian invited.

"You had the door to this vault booby-trapped," Encizo declared. "Maybe that thing is wired, too."

"There's about half a million pesos in that box," Cordova said with a shrug. "Take the money and the cocaine. If you leave now, I'll stall El Tiburón...."

"He thinks we're shaking him down," Encizo said in amusement.

"We don't want your money, Cordova," Katz told the gangster. "Where do you keep the records of your illegal business deals?"

"Records?" Cordova laughed. "You idiots think I keep records of cocaine deals? What are you, DEA? Interpol? Whoever you are, your organization should fire you and hire new people without brain damage."

"Very clever," Katz replied, slipping the strap of the FMK subgun onto his shoulder. "We don't think you have any records about cocaine, but you probably have material on people connected with the trade."

"Like that tame police captain you mentioned in the car," James added, helping himself to the Argentine version of an FAL assault rifle.

"I have nothing of that sort here," Cordova insisted. "Why don't you simply arrest me?"

"We're not going to arrest you," Encizo told him. "We might hand you over to someone who will, though, or we might just kill you instead."

"You'd be wise to cooperate with us," Katz warned. He took a 9 mm Browning from the gun rack. "You're either going to talk for us or die for us. If we weren't honorable men, you'd do both."

Katz emerged from the vault, followed by James and Encizo, who hauled Cordova between them. McCarter and Manning were still standing guard at the office door. They were surprised to see the extra hardware their partners had acquired. Encizo had claimed an FMK-3 submachine gun and a Browning pistol. In addition to the FAL rifle and Sistema Colt, James had taken a Modelo Unico 40 mm grenade launcher, equipped with an FN FAL PARA-style folding stock.

"Looks like you chaps found the candy store," McCarter said with a wolfish grin. "Any goodies left in there?"

"Plenty," Katz assured him. "Get some weapons and lots of ammo."

"Nobody's come near the door," Manning told Katz. "I guess nobody heard your .22 finger gun above the music coming from the lounge. It's pretty loud."

"We have to get out of here now, anyway," the Phoenix Force commander replied. "There's a metal box in the vault. Cordova claims it only contains money. He might be telling the truth, but he could have valuable papers in that thing. Check the box for booby traps. If you suspect it's rigged and you can't deactivate it in a minute or so, leave it."

"I'll take a look at it," the Canadian explosives expert said with a nod.

"Remember, the damn thing isn't vital," Katz urged. "Don't take any risks with it."

Manning followed McCarter into the vault. Encizo easily jimmied the lock to the top drawer of Cordova's desk with a knife blade. He scanned the papers there and sighed with disappointment, then forced the locks of the other drawers and searched the contents.

"Nothing much here," the Cuban announced, leafing through some file folders. "Bookkeeping crap about liquor costs, payroll for club employees... How about that! The limo's a company car. Does that mean you can write it off on your taxes, Cordova?"

"You men could be very rich," the gangster declared with a wild look in his eyes. "I can get you each one million dollars in cash—"

"Shut up, asshole," James said in disgust. "You—"

The office door burst open, the crash drowning James's words, and two gunmen filled the opening. One Colombian killer pointed a machine pistol around the edge of the doorframe while the other dived through the gap and rolled into the room, a cut-down shotgun in his fists.

Neither man managed to fire a single shot.

Yakov Katzenelenbogen nailed the guy at the doorway with a burst of his FMK-3. Four parabellums splintered the doorframe and smashed into the gunman's face. A crimson tide washed the Colombian's features, and he crashed to the corridor floor.

At the same time as Katz, Encizo opened fire with his Browning pistol. He pumped three 9 mm rounds into the tumbling form of the second gunman. He continued to roll until he collided with Cordova's desk. A pool of blood began to form beneath the dead body.

"Hurry up!" Encizo shouted to his partners in the vault. "We've got company!"

12

David McCarter and Gary Manning emerged from the vault, burdened with weapons and ammunition cases. Katz turned to Encizo and cocked his head toward the door. The Cuban nodded. He unslung the FMK from his shoulder and aimed at the office entrance.

Katz and Encizo opened fire. Streams of full-auto projectiles formed an X across the doorway. Slugs slashed into the wall across from the office.

The Israeli held his fire and raised the barrel of the FMK to signal to Encizo that it was safe to advance. The Cuban rushed to the doorway, triggering his subgun as he ran. He poked the muzzle through the gap and fired in the direction the two gunman had come from.

Bullets crashed into three armed figures who huddled low in the hallway, fearful of the barrage of full-auto fire that had just swept the corridor. Encizo hosed the trio with 9 mm rounds. Their bodies jerked from the impact of high-velocity slugs.

Calvin James crouched in the doorway so as not to spoil Encizo's aim. The black commando steadied the

Sistema Colt in both hands and blasted one .45 caliber messenger into the chest of each opponent. The three gunmen were dead when they hit the floor.

"Go!" Encizo shouted as he reloaded the FMK-3 subgun.

Katz shoved Cordova into the corridor with the muzzle of his submachine gun. McCarter and Manning followed, weighed down by weapons and ammo. Encizo and James covered the hallway while the others hustled for the rear exit of Los Extasiar.

Women's screams and men's shouts of surprise echoed from the barroom. In panic, customers and strippers were shoving their way out the front entrance of the club. The bartender and two bouncers, however, had drawn pistols and were moving cautiously toward the corridor.

Though the three men were on Cordova's payroll, they weren't hired guns. They held their pistols in unsteady hands. The bartender poked his head around a corner to peer down the corridor. He cursed when he saw five dead hoodlums on the floor.

He also saw Encizo and James, recognizing them as the two American go-between operators. Though he wasn't sure who they really were, it was obvious that they were now Cordova's enemies and that they meant business with the machine guns they brandished.

Calvin James spotted the bartender and triggered a short salvo of 9 mm rounds at the guy. He purposely aimed above the man's head. Unfamiliar with the Argentine automatic rifle, he didn't want to fire and miss, possibly harming civilians. And besides, the bartender wasn't really a hood. Unless the guy forced his hand, James preferred not to kill him.

Fortunately for all concerned, the bartender and the two bouncers decided not to be heroes. They hurried to follow the customers out the front way.

The other members of Phoenix Force, with Juan Cordova, had already left the club by the back door. James and Encizo followed. All six climbed into the limousine and placed the larger weapons on the floor. Katz sat next to Cordova in the back seat, a pistol jammed against the Colombian's rib cage. James sat on the other side of Cordova, his Gerber knife open in his hand. Across from them, McCarter glowered at the Colombian, his FMK-3 in his lap. Encizo was behind the steering wheel, as usual, and Manning sat next to him.

"Where are we going?" the Cuban asked as he started the engine and shifted into Drive.

"Away from here," Katz answered. "We'll have to get rid of this car as soon as we can. It's too conspicuous. But for now, let's get out of this area before the police arrive."

"What are you planning to do with me?" Cordova demanded, a tremor in his voice betraying his fear.

"We're not taking you to the bloody cinema," McCarter commented gruffly as he slid cartridges into a spare magazine for his subgun. "If we ditch the limo, we'll need another vehicle. Can't be running around with all this firepower strapped to our backs."

"Yeah," James said regretfully, "we'll have to steal another vehicle. I hate ripping off innocent folks."

"We'll just borrow it," Manning said. "Hopefully, it'll still be in one piece when we're through with it."

"We also need a nice quiet place to interrogate Cordova," Katz added. "Head out of the city, Rafael. Let's find some remote area outside of Bogotá."

"I won't talk," the Colombian blustered, but a whine in his tone revealed he wasn't so sure about that. "You can torture me...."

"Don't worry about that," Manning assured him. "Torture not only goes against our principles, it's also too time-consuming. It's unreliable, too, because a man will eventually say anything to stop the pain."

"It's lucky Cordova's hoods didn't confiscate my bankroll," James commented. "We'd better stop at a pharmacy—preferably one without too many customers—and see if we can buy some scopolamine, some morphine and some syringes."

"We use scopolamine," Katz explained to Cordova, "because it's the most reliable truth serum, although it's also very dangerous. It puts a terrible strain on the heart, you know. However, Mr. Wells is an expert in administering this drug. He hasn't lost a patient yet."

"Course, there's always a first time," McCarter commented with a grin.

EL TIBURÓN EMERGED from the archway to the parade field. He cursed under his breath as he pushed his way through the circle of men that surrounded the two combatants in the center of the arena. A floodlight illuminated the battling pair.

The cocaine czar had seen the fight from a window and had hurried outside to try to stop it. One of El Tiburón's men, a Colombian called Vargas, brandished a long-bladed knife at a muscular figure dressed in a jungle camouflage uniform. From the uniform, El Tiburón could tell the other man was a Cuban paratrooper, and he thought he knew who he was.

A glimpse of the Cuban's face confirmed El Tiburón's suspicion. The paratrooper's ruggedly handsome face was marred by a strawberry-colored, heart-shaped birthmark under his right eye. El Tiburón didn't remember the Cuban's name, but he knew he was the captain in charge of training terrorists in small arms and hand-to-hand combat.

Unlike Vargas, the captain didn't have a knife. His open hands were poised at chest level, his feet a shoulders width apart, his knees slightly bent. He shuffled on the balls of his feet, dodging Vargas's knife. The Colombian wielded his blade swiftly, slashing and stabbing, but he struck nothing but air.

"*¡Alto!*" El Tiburón shouted. "Stop it!"

Neither combatant paid heed. Frustrated by his inability to touch the Cuban with his knife, Vargas lunged with a snarl, the blade aimed at the captain's belly. The Cuban sidestepped from the thrusting knife and lashed a kick under the Colombian's extended arm.

The paratrooper's boot slammed into Vargas's lower abdomen. Vargas groaned and folded at the middle. He tried a backhand slash at the captain's belly. A foot-sword kick to the forearm sent the knife spinning from the thug's grasp.

The Colombian was no quitter. He suddenly jumped upright and jabbed a fist at the captain's face. The Cuban parried the punch with a palm stroke and rammed a karate fist to his opponent's solar plexus. Vargas grunted, and the captain swung a karate chop to his temple. The Colombian fell to all fours, stunned by the blow.

Major Pescador jostled his way to El Tiburón's side, winded by his rush to the scene. *"¡Basta!"* he cried. "Enough!"

The Cuban captain heeded his superior officer no more than he had obeyed El Tiburón. With another karate chop, he hit Vargas in the base of the neck. The Colombian fell on his belly. With a *kiai* shout, the captain raised his boot and stomped the heel into the back of his opponent's skull. Several onlookers gasped when they heard bone crunch.

"Lo siento," the captain announced as he snapped to attention. "I am sorry, Comrade Major. I had to complete the contest to the end."

"You disobeyed a direct order, *camarada*," Pescador declared. "That's a court-martial offense. As your commanding officer, I would be within my rights to have you executed for this.''

"*¡Madre de Dios!*" one of El Tiburón's men exclaimed as he knelt beside Vargas's still form. "He's dead! That *cubano cochino* killed him!"

"That's exactly what he said he'd do," a Sandinista in the crowd remarked, clearly impressed by the captain's martial arts prowess.

"What the hell was the meaning of this?" El Tiburón demanded as he approached the two Cuban officers.

"I apologize for killing one of your men," the captain declared. "But Señor Vargas sealed his own doom. For several days he has been mocking me as I trained our comrades in combat skills. At times he was quite abusive. I tolerated his insolence for as long as I could, but tonight he went too far. He insulted our leader of the revolution, Fidel Castro. He said Comrade Castro was a bootlicker of the Soviet Union and compared our leader to Somoza, the former dictator of Nicaragua, who kissed the ass of the hated *yanquis*."

"So you challenged him to a duel?" Major Pescador asked with a frown.

"I reminded him of how he mocked my training in hand-to-hand combat," the captain stated. "He fancied himself as a knife fighter. So I told him I could kill him with my bare hands because his skill with a knife was as feeble as his grasp of politics. Vargas accepted the challenge."

"You did not have to kill him," El Tiburón insisted.

"You are not a *comunista*." The captain sighed. "You do not understand that his insult demanded I take his life. I fought him fairly. I will accept whatever judgment my superior officer decides is proper."

"I'll consider what action to take, Comrade Captain," Major Pescador said wearily. "For now, consider yourself under detention. Stay in your quarters until I contact you."

"Sí, comarada." The captain saluted and marched from the parade field. El Tiburón shook his head grimly as he watched him depart.

"I warned you about that *loco*," the gangster told Pescador. "He's too unstable. I'm not surprised something like this happened, although, you may recall, you assured me the captain would cause no problems."

"What's done is done," Pescador declared. "Let's try to carry on as best we can. Was Vargas popular with your men?"

"He had friends," El Tiburón said with a shrug. "I don't think any of them were terribly close. Vargas also has two brothers. Fortunately for us, they are both in Miami."

"That means they might not return to Colombia," the major commented. "Since that last attempt to ambush the police and federal agents in Miami failed, a lot of your men have been arrested in Florida. In fact, I believe your people have been arrested all over *los Estados Unidos. ¿Veradad?*"

"There have been several arrests," El Tiburón said stiffly. "I'm not sure what went wrong. We had agents within the Miami Vice squad as well as the DEA in Miami. Somehow everything went sour. Details haven't come in yet."

"I was afraid we were trying to do too much too quickly," Pescador said, taking a pack of cigarettes from his tunic pocket. "It was only a matter of time before the police and the *federales* in the United States would put two and two together. I presume you're going to suspend most of your activities in the U.S. until the odds seem a bit more favorable?"

"For now," El Tiburón admitted. He clicked his tongue in disgust as he watched the major light a cigarette.

"You received a radio message today from Bogotá," Pescador stated. "Anything I should know about?"

"Not really," the gangster said with annoyance. "Just a cocaine deal. One of my *tenientes* made contact with some people interested in the purchase of twenty kilos for an overseas market. I take it you've been monitoring my radio frequencies. I go to a lot of trouble to have some privacy, Major. I don't like it being invaded."

"Violating privacy is part of my job," Pescador said simply. "I don't wish to offend you, but as an officer of military intelligence for the Cuban People's Republic—''

El Tiburón interrupted. "Your profession disgusts me, Major."

"That is amusing." Pescador smiled, but his eyes stayed cold and calculating. "You deal in narcotics, smuggling and murder, but you find *my* profession disgusting."

"I apologize," El Tiburón said shortly. He realized the conversation was becoming heated. The Bolivian had formed an alliance with Havana because they shared similar goals, for different motives. Insulting each other would only lead to more friction in an already shaky partnership. "But I'm still distressed about Captain...whatever his name is. What do you intend to do about him, Major?"

"I don't intend to execute him," Pescador replied. "At least not right away. He is very highly trained and a good instructor."

"He's dangerous," El Tiburón insisted.

"That's exactly why we need him," the major said.

"The captain has killed one of my people," the gangster reminded Pescador. "Perhaps he is wonderful at teaching the terrorists...excuse me, the freedom fighters of the world revolution. The fact remains, he killed one of my men on my property. We can't just slap his wrist for that."

"The fight was fair," Pescador stated. "Vargas had a knife."

"Your captain is a trained killer," El Tiburón replied, "skilled in hand-to-hand combat. Vargas was hardly an expert with a knife. You saw him. The fool didn't feint or attempt to distract his opponent. Vargas telegraphed his knife strokes. If I had fought with your captain under the same circumstances, I would have cut him to ribbons, but Vargas didn't have a chance."

"Then he shouldn't have accepted the challenge," the major said with a shrug. "Your man's machismo killed him as much as the fatal blow delivered by Captain—"

"Let's not argue about this," El Tiburón urged, raising his hands in helpless frustration. "We'll worry about your homicidal comrade later. For now, we've got to get some of your beloved guerrillas ready to undertake missions in the outside world."

"Their training is finished," Pescador confirmed. "Have you arranged transportation?"

"The first thing I have to do is get them past the Savajes. If the Indians find them on their own, your men will be cut down by poison darts and arrows before they can get clear of the jungle."

The Savajes were a small primitive tribe, fierce and hostile toward outsiders. Forgotten by time and largely ignored by anthropologists, they lived in much the same way as they had centuries earlier. They were believed to be an offshoot of the Motilones, although the two cultures had few similarities.

El Tiburón had learned about the fierce jungle dwellers from two *zambos* among his men. Half Indian and half black, the *zambos* were at the bottom of the Colombian social ladder. The two *zambos* on El Tiburón's payroll had begun their careers in the cocaine trade by bartering with Indians for coca leaves.

Perhaps curious about the mixed blood of the *zambos*, the Savajes allowed the two to enter their territory unharmed. Communicating by signs and gestures, the *zambos* established trade relations with the suspicious warlike Indians. Through the agency of the *zambos*, El Tiburón, too, began to barter with the tribe. He called them Savajes, Spanish for savages.

Like most Indians of the Amazon and Andes regions, the Savajes chewed coca leaves for hours to achieve the effect of a mild stimulant. They didn't understand why the Bolivian and his followers wanted the leaves badly enough that they would trade merchandise for them.

El Tiburón introduced the Savajes to another drug and made them dependent on him for their supply. The tribe had never learned to ferment organic substances to make alcohol. El Tiburón offered them beer, and later, whiskey. Every week when the booze was delivered, the Indians drank themselves into a stupor. El Tiburón ordered his men to stay out of the jungle on the days immediately following a delivery because the drunken Savajes were unpredictable and more violent than usual.

The Indians sometimes fought with one another during these drunken sprees and occasionally one was killed. But their religion offered an acceptable explanation of such unhappy events. Savajes believed drinking the strange medicine put them in touch with warrior spirits, which banished their fear, pain and worldly care and filled them with a sense of power. If the drink made someone sick, he would vomit spiritual poisons from his body, and that was good. If a fight occurred, the spirits had arranged the contest to establish which man was a better fighter. If someone was killed, that was a judgment of the gods.

Not surprisingly, El Tiburón had helped the Indians develop this bizarre new religion, and he used it to his advantage. The Savajes came to regard him as a holy man with awesome magic. As time passed, his control over the tribe had increased. Few of the Indians realized how the Bolivian had corrupted them. His influence would be needed to guarantee Pescador's men a safe journey.

"After we escort your guerrillas through the jungle," El Tiburón continued, "we'll send them via our smugglers' routes. Safe routes, protected by officials in Colombia, Bolivia, Peru, Panama and elsewhere. We can get your people all the way to Canada if we have to."

"Their destinations are varied," Pescador replied. He had had to listen to El Tiburón's boasts and promises too often. "What matters is that they enter these countries without detection."

"Don't worry about that," El Tiburón assured him with a smile. "But they must also act as mules, delivering cocaine to our operatives and transporting it to Mexico, the Bahamas and, especially, the United States. Then we will all make a profit, and you noble Communist patriots will get your wish . . . to speed up the moral decay of the rotten capitalists."

"Scoff if you like," Major Pescador said grimly. "We take our mission seriously."

"I am very serious when it concerns business," El Tiburón declared. "Deadly serious."

13

General Roberto Torres Castillo lived in a handsome two-story house on the outskirts of Bogotá. The whitewashed adobe dwelling was surrounded by a tall iron fence and guarded around the clock by military police officers. Two sentries were stationed at the front gate. Another pair patrolled the grounds.

The first traces of light in the predawn sky always came as a relief to the sentries on the graveyard shift. It meant their stretch on duty was nearly finished. It meant they had made it through another night without a serious incident. They had survived.

The men at the gate produced a thermos from its concealment behind some bushes and poured themselves some coffee. Their NCOIC had already inspected their post. The soldiers fired up cigarettes and gratefully drew smoke into their lungs as they relaxed.

"*¿Qué es eso?*" one of the sentries whispered as he heard the rattle of a cart against the pavement.

Two men clad in chinos and peasant shirts pulled a two-wheeled cart along the street. They staggered slightly and spoke loudly in slurred Spanish. Clutching the frames of their automatic rifles, the sentries watched the peasants.

"¡Ah, soldados!" Rafael Encizo greeted the guards as he staggered toward the gate. He pushed back his straw sombrero and smiled at them. "Maybe you can help us?"

"We can do nothing for you," one of the soldiers barked. "Get out of here."

"Un momento, por favor," Encizo begged. "My uncle had an accident. His arm fell off...."

"¿Qué?" The other sentry glared at him. "We have no time for such nonsense!"

"You don't understand," Encizo said with a laugh. "It's an artificial arm. My uncle Pedro lost his own arm years ago in a mining accident—digging for emeralds. Anyway, tonight we all drank a little too much and poor Pedro's arm fell off."

Calvin James stumbled from the cart, holding a prosthesis in his hands. The soldiers stared at the metal limb. It had a harness at one end and a hand made of three steel hooks at the other. Then Yakov Katzenelenbogen slid from the cart, too, and staggered forward. He pulled up his empty sleeve to reveal the stump of his right arm.

"Sí." The Israeli pointed at the prosthesis, and slurred his words as he added, "My arm..."

"We know nothing about artificial limbs," the first of the sentries said in a less abrupt tone than before. "You ought to take your uncle to a hospital."

"How did his arm fall off?" the other asked.

"I guess the straps were loose," Encizo replied with a shrug. The sentries turned toward the Cuban and Calvin James, paying little attention to Katz as he leaned against the gate.

"See, the straps are frayed," James pointed out as he pushed the harness end of the prosthesis between two of the gate's iron bars.

"They don't look frayed to me," one guard replied, peering closely at the device.

Moving casually so as not to attract the guards' notice, Katzenelenbogen unclipped a black plastic object from its resting place at the small of his back. He thrust the Nova XR-5000 between the iron bars of the gate and jabbed the hornlike metal prongs under the ribs of the closest sentry. Then Katz pressed the button on the stun gun.

An electrical charge of forty-seven thousand volts gripped the guard. Containing less than one amp, the charge wasn't lethal, but it was temporarily incapacitating. The sentry jerked, stiffened and fell with a groan in a dazed heap.

"*¡Cristo!*" the other guard rasped as he reached for his weapon.

"*Dormirse, amigo,*" Encizo whispered, slipping his arm through the bars to press another XR-5000 stun gun into the guy's chest.

The Cuban fired a nonlethal charge into the second sentry. The soldier groaned as his eyeballs bulged and his mouth fell open. Then he tumbled to the ground beside his companion. Encizo and Katz put their stun guns away.

Calvin James grabbed the fence, hauled himself up the iron bars and hooked a foot onto the top. He vaulted over the summit and dropped to the ground near the two stunned sentries. In a few seconds, James found the controls for the gate and pressed the top button. With an electrical hum, the gate divided in two and slid open.

James bound the wrists and ankles of the sentries with unbreakable plastic riot cuffs and gagged them, while Encizo and Katz pulled the cart through the open gate, closing it behind them. The guards would recover from the electrical shocks within five minutes.

The Phoenix Force men hauled the cart along the drive toward the general's house. The two grounds patrolmen rushed forward, rifles in hand, but not really alarmed. Three peasants with a cart didn't appear to be a threat, and the sentries at the gate hadn't cried out or fired any shots.

"*¡Alto!*" a guard ordered. "*¿Qué hacen Usted?*"

"*¿Qué?*" Encizo replied, raising his arms in surrender.

"*¿Quién es Usted?*" Katz demanded, glaring at the sentries, his arms also raised. The empty sleeve dangled from his abbreviated right arm.

The soldiers were even more puzzled when they looked closely at Katz. They thought a middle-aged, slightly overweight man with only one arm would hardly be accompanying a group of terrorists or *co-quitos*.

While the guards were wondering what was going on, they failed to notice David McCarter and Gary Manning climbing over the fence behind them. The Phoenix Force pair silently crept closer while the guards were still distracted by Katz, Encizo and James.

"Put your weapon on the ground," McCarter rasped as he jammed the muzzle of a Browning pistol into the spine of one of the soldiers.

Manning grabbed the other man from behind and pressed a gun at the back of the guy's neck. The soldiers obeyed the order and placed their rifles on the ground. McCarter and Manning forced the guards to lie on their bellies, then cuffed and gagged them.

"Are you sure we got them all?" Katz inquired as the British and Canadian commandos approached.

"Yeah," Manning confirmed. "The general's security isn't very impressive."

"Let's hope there aren't any surprises inside the house," Katz stated. "So far we've been able to take out Torres's people without harming anyone."

Encizo mounted the steps to the front door. He used the blade of his Gerber knife to probe along the crack near the hinges. The Cuban grunted softly when he felt a wire. A simple burglar alarm, easily deactivated by cutting the wire.

He severed the alarm and checked for other security devices, while the others dragged the unconscious Juan Cordova from the cart. Manning easily slung the sleeping gangster over a brawny shoulder and carried him to the porch.

"There could be a camera or a motion detector on the other side of the door," Encizo told the others as he took a set of lock picks from a pocket. "Or possibly more bodyguards."

"We'll know when you open the door," McCarter replied, stepping to the side of the doorway.

The Cuban inserted two lock picks. "This won't take long. Just a simple double-tumbler lock . . ."

Two clicks confirmed his remark. Encizo turned the knob and pulled the door open.

McCarter promptly jumped across the threshold into a small hallway. He nearly bumped into a military field desk near the door. A startled soldier stared up from behind the desk. He reached for his pistol on the table.

"No, sargento," the Briton warned, noticing the chevrons on the man's sleeve as he pointed his Browning at the NCO's face. "I don't want to kill you. Raise your hands and no one will get hurt."

The sergeant slowly lifted his hands. His eyes darted from McCarter to his own gun on the desk. He breathed hard, stress and fear making his heart beat rapidly. Suddenly he grabbed for the pistol.

"Hell!" McCarter growled as he swatted the barrel of his Browning across the NCO's jaw. The soldier groaned and slid to the floor.

Encizo quickly knelt by the sergeant and cuffed the man's wrists behind his back. The NCO struggled, but

Encizo planted a knee between his shoulder blades to pin him to the floor.

"Relax," the Cuban urged. "If I was a *maleante* or a *terrorista*, I would cut your throat. We just came to talk with the general. He won't be harmed. No one will be harmed."

"The general's wife and children are here," the sergeant said thickly with a split lip. "At least spare them...."

"Do you know Juan Cordova?" Encizo asked, hoping the guy would listen to him instead of jumping to conclusions...not that the Cuban blamed him.

"He sent you?" the NCO inquired.

"We brought him here," Encizo explained, pointing at the unconscious figure draped over Manning's shoulder. "General Torres is an enemy of the *coquitos*. So are we. We're going to help Torres put Cordova behind bars and finish off El Tiburón, the bastard Cordova works for."

Calvin James joined Encizo, kneeling by the overpowered sergeant. "Listen, amigo," he began. "We have to find Torres. If we search the house and startle the general or a member of his family, somebody might get hurt. If we wanted to kill Torres, we wouldn't care how many innocents we had to murder to get him. Do the *coquitos* or *terroristas* care how many innocent lives they have to take?"

"Take us to the general," Encizo urged. "With or without you, we'll find him anyway. If you help us, nobody will get hurt due to a misunderstanding."

"I don't know what I should do..." the NCO admitted.

"Gag him and let's find the general," Katz said sharply. "We've spent too long trying to convince this man."

"Very well," the sergeant said. "I'll take you to General Torres."

The sergeant led Phoenix Force up a flight of stairs and tilted his head toward the door to the master bedroom. Encizo knocked twice, then hammered his fist against the door.

"*¿Quién llama?*" a man's voice demanded from the room within.

"Sergeant Santos," the NCO replied. "Some men have come to see you. They claim to have apprehended Juan Cordova and brought him here for you."

"*¿Qué?*" the man within said with astonishment. "What sort of nonsense is this? *Un momento.* I'll have words with you, Sergeant."

The door opened, and a heavyset man appeared, a .45 caliber pistol in his fist. The general's hair was white, and folds of flesh hung from his jawline, but his eyes looked at least ten years younger than his body He stared defiantly at the men of Phoenix Force.

Encizo greeted him with a bow. "General Torres, we apologize for this intrusion, but we had to make cer tain our meeting was confidential."

"How did you get in?" Torres demanded. "My guards..."

"We tied them up and gagged them," the Cuban explained. "This is important, General. *Por favor*, hear what we have to say."

"We'll talk in my study," Torres said gruffly. He put his pistol in the pocket of his dressing gown and pointed at Cordova, who was still draped across Manning's shoulder. "Bring that thing with you."

The general led them to a large room lined with bookcases. He walked to a bar and poured himself some brandy in a balloon glass. His confident manner showed he was accustomed to giving orders. He seemed to take the unexpected visit in stride, as if gun-toting intruders were a routine event. As Manning dumped the unconscious Cordova on the carpet, Torres sized up each member of Phoenix Force in turn with an assessing stare.

"You men aren't Colombians," Torres commented at last, sipping his brandy. "What are you? *¿Norteamericanos?* DEA? CIA?"

"We're on the same side as you are," James assured him. "That's all that matters. We've just spent four hours squeezing information out of Cordova. He was under the influence of scopolamine, so he told us the truth."

"Scopolamine?" Torres glared at the black man. "You fellows have broken the law of my country—"

"The *coquitos* don't play by the rules, either, General," Encizo interrupted. "And they're way ahead of you people who are constrained by the law. In fact, some of your fellow officers in the Colom-

bian army are in El Tiburón's pocket. Cordova told us
about a number of high-ranking military and government personnel who are bent worse than a crippled
camel. He also told us you couldn't be bought off or
blackmailed. That's why we're here."

"You mention El Tiburón." The general frowned.
"What does the Shark have to do with this?"

"Cordova was one of his lieutenants," Encizo explained, taking two cassette tapes from his pocket.
"The information on these tapes was recorded while
Cordova was chatting with us, with the help of truth
serum."

"We can't use anything on those tapes in court,"
Torres said with a sigh. "Just as in the United States,
a confession made under such circumstances is
worthless."

"But the information itself isn't," James assured
him. "Cordova spilled his guts about lots of people
and lots of crooked operations. You've got enough
here to arrest a whole bunch of *coquitos* and the low-
lifes who've been working for them. You can claim
some reliable sources gave you some good tips. When
you make the busts, you'll find the evidence you need
to fry the bastards."

"What about Cordova?" Torres inquired, looking
down at the insensible gangster.

"I shot him up with morphine," James answered
with a shrug. "He'll be on cloud nine for at least another hour. Don't worry, he can't hear a thing."

"I meant, what do you expect me to do with him?" Torres asked. "I can't hold him without laying legal charges, and your proof isn't admissible in court."

"Just explain the facts of life to him," Encizo suggested. "Tell him that when people start getting burned because they knew him, the syndicate is bound to figure he turned informer. His life won't be worth a forged peso after that. So he can either turn informer for real, or take his chances with the *coquitos*."

"Hell," McCarter added, "we can take the bastard with us and dump him somewhere on the street. He'll wake up and wonder what really happened and what was just a dream when he was flying on morphine. By the time he figures it out, it'll be too late. Once the arrests begin, Cordova will have to turn himself in and volunteer to turn state's witness, or his own kind will take care of him for us. Either way, he's finished."

Torres smiled in reluctant admiration. "You fellows are diabolical. I'm glad you're on our side. Do these tapes have anything that will help us get El Tiburón himself?"

"They do," Encizo confirmed. "But we'll take care of the Shark. You can help—"

Torres interrupted. "You five have already broken enough laws," he snapped. "You're not going to carry out any more vigilante justice in my country."

"General, let me lay this out for you," McCarter said persuasively. "El Tiburón has teamed up with some agents from Havana. They're training terrorists at his base. In a couple of days the bastards are going to be slithering out of the jungle, transporting cocaine and carrying out missions of violence against your country and a number of others in South America. Not to mention Central America, Mexico and the United States. There isn't time to go through regular channels. We've got to find El Tiburón's base and destroy it.''

''Just you five?'' Torres scoffed. ''That's crazy.''

''Not as crazy as trying to do it with Colombian soldiers, half of whom might be working for the *coquitos*,'' Encizo answered. ''We're going to do this more or less on our own, but you could help if you're willing, General.''

''What do you have in mind?'' Torres asked, sighing resignedly.

''We need clothing for jungle combat,'' Encizo replied. ''And other gear, weapons and ammunition if possible . . . and a guide who knows the jungle. Somebody who can take us to the area known as *la Guarida de Diablo*.''

''You want to go to the Devil's Lair?'' The general stared at them as if all five had to be insane. ''That place is well named. People go in there and are never heard of again. It is very dangerous.''

''So are we, General,'' McCarter assured him, ''so are we.''

14

El Tiburón and Major Pescador strolled through the cocaine refinery on their daily inspection tour. The refinery was located half a mile from the walls of the fortress. Trucks and rebuilt World War II airplanes regularly transported clear plastic bags full of coca leaves from the highlands of the Andes where the bushes grew to the refinery where the leaves were processed.

All the stages of the processing were taking place as El Tiburón and the Cuban officer inspected the refinery. They paused to observe half a dozen workers "salting" coca leaves in a large bin. The peasants added powdered carbonate to the bin, stirring and tossing the contents by hand as if preparing a huge salad. The salting process softened the alkaloid within the leaves.

Large quantities of coca leaves that had already been salted were spread out on cheesecloth nets stretched between two trees. After "sweating" there in the sun for three to five hours, the leaves would be soaked in kerosene or gasoline for approximately thirty-six hours. The gasoline or kerosene drew out the alkaloid that was the coca base for cocaine. Nearby, a press squeezed the liquid out of the sodden leaves.

Other workers were mixing water with acid and adding it to the liquid containing the alkaloid to produce guarapo. The guarapo was then mixed with water in barrels and stirred for roughly half an hour. That mixture was poured into large jars and left standing for twenty-four hours to allow the alkaloid solution to settle to the bottom.

Again El Tiburón and Pescador stopped briefly to watch the next step in the manufacture of cocaine. Two workers were adding liquid ammonia to a bottle that had been filled with guarapo and water the previous day. The ammonia produced a milky substance. The coca guarapo was then ready to be filtered through cheesecloth. The solid that remained on the cloth was called coca base. It was set to dry in the sun. At night it would be dried under sunlamps in the refinery greenhouse.

The process up to the point of producing coca base was simple and required no sophisticated equipment or expertise in chemistry. The product was called coca paste, when it was distributed in this unrefined form, and it was much less expensive than cocaine.

Smoking coca paste cigarettes was a common and very dangerous form of drug abuse in South America among low-income groups. In Bolivia, enough coca paste for one hundred cigarettes could be purchased for about seventy-five cents. One gram of the paste sold for twenty dollars; if further refined into pure cocaine, that single gram would be worth two thousand dollars.

Transforming coca base into pure cocaine required far more expertise and care than the early stages of production. In El Tiburón's main laboratory, the head chemist, Miguel Napoli Leguizamo, was supervising the final phases of the process. In one area, technicians were carefully combining the coca base with a mixture of acetone and highly flammable ether. El Tiburón and Major Pescador found Napoli himself adding hydrochloric acid to coca base. This, too, was very risky.

Napoli was a master of rationalization. He claimed that he was more interested in research than money, that he hoped to develop safer, less addictive cocaine. He told himself he was no different from the chemists who supervised the fermentation of alcohol for big liquor companies. He also spoke about supply and demand to anyone who questioned his calling. If Napoli didn't help to process cocaine, someone else would do it. Why shouldn't he be the one to make the profit? he asked himself whenever doubts about his involvement in a criminal business assailed him. He would use the money for his family, for his children's education. He wasn't a criminal. He didn't force anyone to buy cocaine. He didn't sell it. Napoli had many excuses, and he was always desperately seeking new ones.

He looked up as El Tiburón and Pescador approached. *"Buenos días, jefe,"* he said, setting down the container of acid and slipping on his wire-rimmed glasses. "How are you this morning?"

"Fine, Miguel," El Tiburón replied. "Production of merchandise seems to be coming along nicely. How much cocaine is ready to go?"

"Two hundred and fifty kilos," Napoli answered, patting one of the large glass bottles that contained coca base mixed with other chemicals. "And this batch will be ready in a few hours. Then we'll have another one hundred and fifty kilos of pure cocaine."

"That's four hundred," Pescador said with a frown as he took a pack of cigarettes from his pocket. "I thought our people would get five hundred—"

"Don't light a cigarette in here," Napoli warned abruptly. He pointed at several drums of ether. "You could blow us all to hell."

"We have more cocaine," El Tiburón assured Pescador. "Don't worry. Your people will get the full five hundred kilos. After all, distributing cocaine is my business."

"We'll have another hundred or perhaps two hundred kilos by tomorrow morning if we work double shifts," Napoli stated. "We'll have to use sunlamps for the coca base, and the workers will have to be paid extra, though."

"You have a lot of laborers," the Cuban remarked, tilting his head toward the workers outside the lab. "Where do you get them from?"

"That's easy," El Tiburón answered. "Most of them used to work for the rubber plantations. The price of rubber has not increased as much as the costs involved in growing rubber trees and cutting, processing and transporting the products. A lot of former rubber workers have turned to the cocaine business. The work is easier and the money is much better. Eh, Miguel?"

"The money is good," Napoli agreed. "But for a chemist, the job isn't easy. I work with many dangerous substances, you know. It is not good for my nerves."

"Ah, but you can afford some expensive forms of relaxation after this job is over." The *coquito* laughed as he slapped Napoli on the back. "Soon your work will be finished and you can take a nice long vacation in Madrid."

"Paris, France," Napoli said with a smile.

"So, Major," El Tiburón said, turning to Pescador, "your people will have their cocaine and can get on with their mission to spread its corruption to the diseased minions of the imperialist *yanquis*."

"The sooner the better," Pescador said emphatically.

ALBERTO FERN SLASHED his machete through the tangled vines of the jungle. A wiry man with whipcord muscles, Alberto hacked a path just wide enough for his compact body. The big men behind him would enlarge the passage for themselves.

Rafael Encizo swung his machete to slice away more brush. Gary Manning was next in line and cleaved through more foliage with powerful strokes of his jungle knife. Katz, McCarter and James followed. They only needed to push aside a few vines and branches to follow the others into the brush.

"How you like the jungle so far?" Alberto inquired, grinning through his drooping black mustache. The wiry Colombian continued to slash away foliage as he spoke.

"Can't recall when I've had more fun," Calvin James replied, swatting a mosquito against his neck. "How much farther to the Devil's Lair?"

"*La Guarida de Diablo* is a few more kilometers," the guide assured him. "I think we rest for a while, no?"

"Yes," Manning said dryly as he lowered himself to the ground and stuck his machete in the earth next to his right knee.

"You hombres are doin' okay," Alberto announced. He wiped the back of a hand across his sweat-drenched forehead. "You all in pretty good shape for gringos. Even you, old one."

"The old one might be a bit stiff tomorrow morning," Yakov Katzenelenbogen admitted, sounding ever so slightly winded as he sat opposite the guide. "General Torres didn't tell us much about you, Alberto."

"Didn't tell me much about you, either," the guide said with a shrug.

"That's because he doesn't know much about us," David McCarter explained, taking a canteen from his belt. "Torres told us you know the Amazon jungle better than most who actually live in it."

"I used to live here," Alberto declared proudly. "I was born and raised in a Chibcha village near the great river. You know, the Chibcha once had a great empire in Colombia before the Spanish came. At San Agustín, you can see for yourself the great statues built by my ancestors. Three thousand years those stone figures have stood. Some say they look like the work of the Maya or the Aztecs. The whites will tell you no one knows who built those statues, but *I* tell you it was the Chibcha who did this."

"How'd you meet up with General Torres?" Encizo inquired, drawing a K-Bar Combat Bowie from its belt sheath. He stroked the blade against a whetstone to hone the edge.

"How'd *you* meet him?" the guide replied.

"We broke into his house just before dawn," Calvin James answered with a shrug. The black commando sat cross-legged on the ground and placed an M-16 assault rifle across his lap. "Guess we charmed his socks off."

"Sure." Alberto scoffed. "Oh, well, I met the general a few years ago when I was helping the army find people who got lost in the jungle. He asked me what I thought of the *coquitos* and I said I thought they should have their fuckin' heads cut off in public. General Torres said that wasn't possible just yet, but he'd like to use me to track down jungle laboratories where the *coquitos* make cocaine.''

"Ever go after any of the bastards in the Devil's Lair?" McCarter asked, lighting a Player's cigarette.

"No way," Alberto replied. He liked to show off his mastery of American slang. "I've been to the Devil's Lair one time and I hoped I would never go back there."

"What happened?" Manning asked.

"I was with a patrol of soldiers," Alberto began, tracing an aimless pattern on the ground with a stick. "We were checking a rumor about *coquitos* in the area. We were attacked with no warning. Two soldiers screamed in much pain. I saw them fall. One had been shot in the chest with three arrows. The other had three or four darts sticking in his face. One dart had struck him in the eye. Blood from his eye was pouring down his cheek."

"Darts?" James raised his eyebrows. "You mean like *poison darts* from blowguns?"

"Yes. The Indians fired darts and arrows at us from all directions. A few of them had firearms, but their aim was better with the primitive weapons. We fired back at the Indians. We could just see fleeting shapes in the bushes. I don't know if we hit one of them, but they sure hit us. We lost more than half our patrol."

"General Torres told us that people go into the Devil's Lair and don't come out," Manning commented.

"Just like the Bates Motel," James added.

"One of the hoodlums in Miami also mentioned hostile Indians who live in the jungle surrounding El Tiburón's fortress," Katz recalled. "The fellow said they were 'cannibals' or 'headhunters' or something like that."

"I don't think they are cannibals," Alberto answered. "The Jivaro Indians in Peru and Ecuador used to be headhunters. Maybe some of them still are. I don't know if the tribe we have to worry about are headhunters or not. They could be related to the Jivaro. Nobody knows anything about them except that they're dangerous. We don't even know what to call the tribe. Some have called them the Savajes because that's the only Spanish word any of them have ever been heard to say."

"Maybe they were calling the intruders 'savages,'" McCarter suggested. "It is sort of a relative term. A lot of Westerners would consider a military firing squad to be 'civilized capital punishment,' but they'd condemn a public execution by decapitation in Saudi Arabia as 'savage behavior.'"

"I think Savajes is a good name for the tribe," Alberto stated, taking some beef jerky from a pouch on his belt. "Of course, they shot poison darts at me. I'm an Indian, too, but my people don't try to kill anyone who gets near their territory. I can understand why Indians feel unfriendly toward other Colombians. But that doesn't excuse what the Savajes do."

"They were probably victimized a lot in the past," Katz mused, puffing on a Camel cigarette. "The tribe would become isolated, distrustful of others, withdrawn. It would be interesting to study them in detail. From what you've told me, the 'savages' are probably living in much the same manner as they have for hundreds of years.''

Yakov Katzenelenbogen had more than a layman's interest in anthropology. He had studied the history and development of man in the Middle East.

"You realize we won't get an opportunity to study these Indians," Manning told Katz. "We'll be lucky if we don't run into them. If we do, they'll be trying to kill us and . . ."

"We'll have to take appropriate action." Katz sighed. "I know. The Indians have been corrupted by El Tiburón. They're on his side, and that makes them our enemies. It's unfortunate, but armies clash on battlefields and strangers are forced to kill one another under similar circumstances. That's the nature of war and, like it or not, we're at war with El Tiburón.''

"I do sort of like it," McCarter said with a grin.

"Me, too," Alberto said, grinning. "The Shark is one of the most powerful *coquitos* in South America. He should have been put down long ago. I'm glad that I can help finish that bastard once and for all."

"Well, that's what we're here for," Manning said.

The Canadian still carried one of the Argentine FAL assault rifles they had taken from Juan Cordova's vault at the Bogotá nightclub. General Torres had provided a Bushnell scope for the rifle. He had also supplied Manning with seven kilos of C-4 plastic explosives, plus detonators and special blasting caps.

Calvin James carried an M-16, which had also been supplied by Torres. The general hadn't been able to find an M-203 grenade launcher attachment, so James also carried the Modelo Unico 40 mm launcher taken from Cordova's vault. He had the .45 caliber Sistema Colt confiscated from the vault as well.

Torres hadn't been able to supply Katz with an Uzi, McCarter with a MAC-10 Ingram or Encizo with a Heckler and Koch MP-5 machine pistol. All three men still carried FMK-3 submachine guns "liberated" from the armory adjacent to Cordova's office. The Argentine weapon was a cross between an Uzi and an M-3 "grease gun." It was similar to the weapons the trio usually carried, and it fired 9 mm parabellum ammo.

The general had contributed extra 9 mm ammo as well as some 40 mm cartridge-style grenades for the launchers James and Encizo carried. In addition to guns and ammunition, Torres had rounded up camouflage fatigue uniforms, paratrooper boots, K-Bar Combat knives, LRP survival rations, canteens, compasses and backpacks. He had even located a Barnett Wildcat crossbow and a dozen bolts for McCarter. The Briton favored the Barnett Commando bow with folding stock and cocking lever, but the Wildcat was a top-quality crossbow. Torres had included a scope for the weapon.

The general had even managed to come up with twenty M-59 hand grenades and five concussion grenades. The men of Phoenix Force still carried the Browning pistols and Sistema Colt taken from Cordova's vault, but Torres had supplied shoulder holsters for the handguns.

The five warriors also carried walkie-talkies. These could be used to communicate with one another if they were forced to separate, or to contact General Torres. The Colombian officer had arranged to send a helicopter to airlift them out after their mission was accomplished.

The most useful contribution Torres had made to the mission, however, was Alberto. Without the guide, Phoenix Force would have been lost before even setting foot in the jungle.

The Colombian tropical rain forest was formidable. A great variety of trees grew in the region, including such commercially valuable ones as mahogany, oak, cedar and coconut palm. A riot of orchids, hyacinth, jasmine and other flowers decorated the green walls of the jungle. Monkeys chattered and parrots cawed among the branches of the trees.

As Alberto led Phoenix Force farther into the jungle, they approached a stream surrounded by dense ferns. The guide suddenly stopped and held a finger to his lips, urging the others to be silent. He pointed at two large shapes on the opposite side of the stream.

A muscular seven-foot spotted jaguar and a slightly smaller black one waded into the water. Most cats objected to getting their fur wet, but jaguars frequently swam and frolicked in rivers and streams. Of all the jungle felines, only jaguars and tigers willingly entered water to swim and to cool themselves in the heat of the afternoon.

The big cats sensed the presence of the men. They swiftly leaped from the stream and vanished into the jungle. Alberto smiled at his companions and resumed swinging his machete at the vines and brush. After squeezing through a gap, he stepped over a log.

Alberto gasped and staggered backward from the log. Encizo moved forward, machete raised. Guessing Alberto had been startled by a poisonous snake, Encizo was prepared to strike at it. He didn't expect to see what was on the other side of the log.

The remains of a human body lay on the ground. Now only a skeleton clad in rotten rags of clothing, the body appeared to have been there for more than a month. Animals and insects had picked the bones clean of flesh, but the large hole in the center of the skull clearly revealed the cause of death. Animals didn't wield hatchets or war clubs.

"I think we're getting closer to the Savajes," Alberto said, unable to repress a shudder.

15

The jungle seemed to extend to infinity. Plants and vines barred the path, and long tree roots jutted from the ground like animal snares. Hungry mosquitos and deer flies assaulted the team. The men were afraid to swat the insects, fearful that the sound of a slap might betray their presence to the hostile Indians. They squashed the blood-sucking insects against their flesh and wiped the crimson and green smears on their trousers.

"God," McCarter rasped, wiping a crushed tick from his palm. "These little buggers are going to suck us dry before we find El Tiburón."

"I'd almost welcome coming up against opponents who can be shot," James added, squashing a mosquito against his neck.

Encizo tripped over a vine and sprawled forward on his hands and knees. If he hadn't fallen, no one would have given the log a second look. Encizo grabbed Alberto's leg just as the guide was about to step over the log, holding him back and crying, "Wait a minute!"

The Cuban pointed to one end of the log. It had been chopped by an ax. There was no corresponding stump anywhere nearby. Alberto raised his eyebrows and nodded as he stepped back.

"Somebody put this leg here for a purpose," Manning whispered as he knelt by the hacked-off end. The grass in the immediate area was slightly bent and not quite as tall as the surrounding blades. "It must have been dragged here in the last couple of days."

Encizo picked up a rock as large as a man's skull. He estimated that it weighed about eight kilos. He gestured for the others to get back, then hurled the stone so that it hit the ground on the other side of the log. Then he ducked, covering his head in case the rock detonated an antipersonnel mine.

There was no explosion, but the stone disappeared along with an area of jungle floor about five feet in diameter. Encizo peered over the log into a pit about six feet deep, with several wooden stakes sticking up from the bottom. The ends had been sharpened and were stained with a black substance. The pit had apparently been covered with a cloth of some kind, camouflaged by a layer of earth and pebbles to look like solid ground. The stakes were so sharp, they had penetrated the cloth when it fell on them weighted by the rock.

"I'm glad you were alert, amigo," Alberto told Encizo, staring at the deadly mantrap. "I owe you my life."

"Don't worry about that," the Cuban replied. "But we'd better keep an eye peeled for more booby-traps. The Savajes haven't exactly rolled out the red carpet to welcome us!"

Just then Katz saw the branches of a bush part as a long pointed stick appeared among the leaves. "Down!" he shouted.

They all threw themselves to the ground. A hail of flying arrows from the surrounding jungle sliced the air above them. One arrow struck the ground less than an inch from Gary Manning's head. Others slashed into the bushes behind them.

"Shit," Calvin James rasped through clenched teeth. "Where are the bastards?"

"Don't ask me," Katz replied, bracing his FMK-3 across his prosthesis. "I only saw one of them."

"I think there's more than that out there," Manning commented as he pointed his FAL in the direction that most of the arrows seemed to come from.

McCarter sprayed the jungle on all sides with 9 mm rounds, moving his Argentine subgun from left to right. Bullets raked the brush. Voices screamed in agony, and the bloodied bodies of two Savaje Indians tumbled into view. Small and painfully thin, the copper-brown bodies were naked except for loincloths that barely covered the crotch area.

The Indians were obviously dead. However, dozens of survivors darted through the dense foliage. James opened fire with his M-16, blasting a stream of 5.56 mm rounds into the path of two fleeing Savajes.

Leaves flew as they were sheared from the stems of plants. The Indians threw up their arms as they howled and toppled to the ground.

"Man," Calvin James rasped through clenched teeth, "this reminds me of Vietnam."

"Yeah," Manning agreed as he searched the jungle through the Bushnell scope of his rifle.

A Savaje ambusher raised his head and peered between the branches of a stout rubber tree. Long black hair framed his face. His features were flat, with stern dark eyes and a broad full mouth. The Indian's bow bisected his face as he prepared to launch an arrow.

Manning squeezed the trigger of the FAL. A 7.62 mm slug rocketed from the barrel and split the bow in two. The high-velocity projectile crashed into the Savaje's forehead, drilled through his brain and exploded through a gory exit wound at the base of his skull.

Well aware that the attack would come from all directions, Katz, Encizo and Alberto turned to cover the other angles. Plants rustled as Savajes hurried into position. The Israeli and Cuban commandos fired their FMK-3 chatterguns. Parabellums chewed away chunks of foliage and slammed the life from at least five opponents.

Alberto was armed with a pump shotgun, devastating at close range, but virtually useless beyond a limited distance, and a 9 mm Star Model 28 autoloader. He snapped off the safety catch of the autoloader and fired three rounds at a clump of ferns that moved slightly.

His effort failed to claim a human target. Instead, a Savaje warrior rose from behind the plant. He held a long wooden tube in his fists, placing one end at his lips and the other pointed at Alberto. Desperate, the guide fired two more rounds at the Indian.

A parabellum slug hit the Savaje in the belly. He doubled up from the impact of the bullet as he exhaled into the blowpipe. A poison-tipped dart spat from the wooden muzzle but landed harmlessly in front of the wounded Indian. The Savaje crumpled into a moaning ball of pain, both arms clutched to his bullet-torn abdomen.

Arrows and darts whistled through the air. The five men of Phoenix Force and their guide sought cover behind some nearby trees. Projectiles struck bark. A poison dart penetrated the side of Encizo's backpack near his right shoulder.

With a steel hook of his prosthesis, Katz yanked out the pin of a concussion grenade and hurled the blaster at the enemy. Manning followed the Israeli's example with an M-59 frag grenade, lobbing his explosive egg at another group of Savajes to the east.

The grenades exploded. Bodies were flung from the cover of foliage. Three Indians staggered into the open, their hands clamped to their skulls, eardrums shattered by the concussion blast. Two others were torn apart by the fragger. Another Savaje stumbled into view, blood flowing from the ragged stump at his right shoulder where his arm had once been.

Many Indians bolted from the explosions. McCarter and Encizo fired their FMK-3 subguns into the dashing shapes. Savajes screamed and fell like tenpins struck by a huge invisible bowling ball. Only a few Indians now fired arrows or blowgun darts in response. Their aim was poor, and none of these projectiles landed closer than a yard from Phoenix Force. The explosions had clearly disoriented their primitive opponents.

A large-caliber bullet smashed into a tree trunk above McCarter's head. The roar of the weapon echoed above the chatter of automatic fire. McCarter saw smoke rise from the barrel of an old Mauser-style rifle that jutted from some cinchona shrubs. He promptly sprayed the bushes with 9 mm slugs. The Mauser fell from the cinchona, and its owner dropped dead.

"Not very good with guns, are they?" the Briton commented.

A dart sizzled past Calvin James's face, barely missing the tip of his nose. Startled by the projectile, the black man threw his head back. The dart struck in a low-hanging branch of a nearby oak.

"But they're pretty fuckin' good with those blowguns," James commented as he swung his M-16 toward the attacker.

He scanned the area for the guy with the blowgun, but couldn't find the bastard. Then movement in the leaves high in a tree caught his eye. He gazed up at a Savaje fitting a dart into the end of a wooden tube.

"Welcome to the twentieth century," James snarled as he raised the automatic rifle and fired a three-round burst.

The 5.56 mm hornets tore into the Indian and kicked him out of the tree. The Savaje screamed as he plunged to the ground twelve feet below, landing with a sickening crunch. His spine snapped when he hit the ground.

Many of the Savajes had fled from the battlefield, terrified by the fearsome firepower and deadly skills of Phoenix Force. Others still stood their ground and continued to launch arrows and blowgun darts at the commandos. Veterans of hundreds of gun battles, the five-man army functioned with professional efficiency. While Katz and McCarter reloaded, James and Encizo fired at the enemy to keep the Indians pinned down.

Blowguns and arrows were very accurate in the hands of experts, but they required a clear target and ample time to aim, fire and reload. The steady barrage of full-auto rounds forced the Indians to stay low, which made it difficult for them to use their traditional weapons.

The Savajes armed with outdated Mauser rifles proved to be terrible marksmen. El Tiburón had supplied them with little ammunition, fearful they might turn against him. None of the Indians had developed skill with the Mausers. They were unfamiliar with the recoil, and some of them were afraid of firing the weapons. When they pulled the triggers, they closed their eyes or flinched so badly their bullets were several feet off target.

Two rifle-toting Savajes charged forward, apparently believing their firearms made them invincible. They took too long aiming their weapons and Phoenix Force cut them down like stalks of sugarcane under the blade of a machete. James and Encizo reloaded their weapons while Katz and McCarter covered them.

Manning fired his FAL on semiauto, using the telescopic sights to pick off the position of opponents beyond the range of submachine guns. Although many of the Indians were highly skilled at camouflage and at hunting big game, Manning, too, was a hunter. He had stalked deer in Canada as a boy, and men in the jungles of Vietnam. Manning was an expert at finding his quarry regardless of the terrain.

The Canadian's FAL roared when the cross hairs of his scope defined a target. The powerful 7.62 mm slugs shattered faces and blasted apart skulls. Though the Savajes had encountered modern weapons before, they had never pitted themselves against opponents as skillful and well trained as the men of Phoenix Force.

More than a dozen Indians had already been killed. Others, having exhausted their supply of arrows and darts, took advantage of an honorable reason to retreat. A few were possessed by the frenzy of battle. They charged with machetes and spears in their fists.

Two spear-wielding Savajes attacked Calvin James. One charged at James, his body low with his lance held in front of his bowed head. The other Indian balanced his spear and cocked it back to his ear, ready to throw. The projectile weapon presented the more immediate threat. James fired a three-round burst into the torso of the Savaje before he could hurl his lance.

By then the other Indian was closing in. James swung his M-16 toward the second opponent, but the Savaje lunged for James's belly. With lightning speed, the black warrior slammed the barrel of his assault rifle across the shaft of the spear and stepped aside. The lance stabbed air near James's left hip.

James launched a high roundhouse kick. The steel toe of his paratrooper boot crashed into the Savaje's skull at the jawbone joint under the ear. The Indian's head snapped to the side. He dropped his lance and collapsed in a heap.

Alberto's shotgun bellowed, and a burst of buckshot slammed through the chest of a machete-wielding Savaje. Another Indian hurled a spear at Gary Manning. The Canadian dodged the missile, and its flint tip pierced the bark of an oak behind him. The shaft wobbled on impact, its spearhead buried in the trunk.

Yet another Indian attacked Manning, jungle knife clenched in a two-handed grip. The Canadian pointed his FAL at the man's chest and squeezed the trigger. A dull click announced that he had burned up all his ammo. Manning dropped the empty rifle, turned swiftly and in a single fluid motion yanked the spear from the tree trunk. The flint point, however, remained firmly lodged in the bark.

The machete-wielding opponent swung his weapon at Manning's skull. The Phoenix pro lashed out with the spear shaft. The pole struck the Savaje's wrists and sent the machete hurtling from numb fingers. Manning quickly reversed his grip and whipped the shaft between the Indian's legs. The Savaje gasped in agony as the blow crushed his testicles. He fell to his knees, both hands clutching the loincloth at his crotch. Manning clubbed the Indian across the side of the head, knocking him unconscious.

Five Savajes charged toward Katz and Encizo. The Phoenix pair sprayed the attackers with FMK-3 bullets. Three Indians fell, dying, but the other two closed quarters and attacked. One of them thrust a lance at Encizo's belly.

The Cuban dodged the spearhead, but the Indian swiftly swung the butt of the lance at Encizo, knocking the submachine gun from his hands. The Phoenix fighter pivoted, spinning away from his opponent and drawing his machete from its scabbard. The Indian lunged. Encizo slashed with the jungle knife and the powerful stroke chopped through the shaft of the spear above the flint tip.

The startled Indian reacted quickly and swung the shaft at Encizo's head. The Cuban ducked under the whirling stick and lunged with his machete. The tip of the large knife pierced flesh under the Savaje's breastbone and stabbed upward into his heart. He opened his mouth to scream, and a torrent of blood spilled across his chest.

The last Savaje attacker charged at Katz with a war club raised at shoulder level. The Israeli had no time to swing the FMK-3 into position. Instead, he stepped forward and raised his prosthesis before the Indian could swing his weapon.

The steel hooks of the prosthesis clamped around the Savaje's wrist. The Indian's eyes swelled with astonishment, and his mouth fell open as he stared at the metal talons that gripped his arm. The war club fell from trembling fingers. The terrified Indian shrieked with fear as he tried to break free of Katz's steel grasp.

"Go!" Katz shouted. He released the Savaje's wrist and pushed him away. The Indian ran from the commandos, gibbering what might have been desperate prayers.

"I guess he never saw an artificial hand before," Alberto said with a grin. "Probably thinks you're some sort of wizard."

"As long as he stays away and convinces his comrades to do likewise," the Israeli remarked.

Indeed, the Savajes had withdrawn, leaving behind several slain warriors on the floor of the jungle. The members of Phoenix Force reloaded their weapons. McCarter fired up a Player's and drew smoke deep into his lungs.

"Well," the Briton said with a sigh, "that was a nasty little exercise in violence."

"Yeah," Encizo agreed. "But we haven't found El Tiburón yet. This fight with the Indians may be a cakewalk compared to what's waiting for us at the Shark's fortress."

16

"El Tiburón!" Major Pescador exclaimed as he stomped into the Bolivian's office. "I just received a radio message from Captain—"

"I also received a message from the jungle refinery," El Tiburón replied. He stood by a window, gazing out at the blue-and-gold sky. The *coquito* didn't bother to turn and face Pescador. "I know what you are about to say. They heard gunshots in the region of the Savajes."

"Automatic fire," the Cuban intelligence officer corrected. "And explosions, possibly grenades. The Indians must have clashed with a large and well-armed unit of soldiers. Perhaps an assault force."

"The Savajes have encountered patrols of soldiers in the past," El Tiburón told him, still staring at the predusk sky. "They have always repelled the invaders, and there is no reason to believe they failed this time."

"You can't be certain they succeeded, either," Pescador insisted. "Too much is at stake for us to be overconfident."

"Or for us to panic and overreact to a situation that probably doesn't threaten us in the first place," El Tiburón stated as he turned from the window. "I've been involved in this business most of my life, Major. One must have a proper balance. Too much caution can be almost as dangerous as too little."

"Gangster philosophy?" Pescador said with contempt. "I'm not impressed. Our operation doesn't just concern your damned cocaine, El Tiburón. It concerns the interests of Havana . . . not just the Colombian syndicate or MERGE. I will not have this mission jeopardized because you believe a bunch of backward savages can fight off soldiers armed with modern weapons."

"Even if there is an assault force headed our way," El Tiburón began, his voice as calm as his impassive face, "they still won't be able to take this fortress. I have a small army here."

"Perhaps they sent an army to attack you," the Cuban suggested. "Anything is possible, *señor*. Your security could have been violated when the authorities seized your lieutenant in Bogotá."

"You've been listening in on my radio messages again," El Tiburón remarked, his eyes narrowing with anger. "Frankly, Major, I shall be glad when you, your soldiers, your Sandinistas and your guerrilla fighters have all left."

"What do you intend to do about the incident in the jungle?" Pescador demanded.

"The government couldn't organize a large assault force in less than a day without my informers sending word to me," El Tiburón stated. "No swarm of soldiers and police is closing in on us. Besides, a large unit of men cannot approach without being spotted long before they reach the fortress. In an emergency, we can abandon this site and escape in helicopters while our men hold off the invaders."

"So you plan to simply ignore the danger and hope it isn't serious?" Pescador glared at him. "I say we should find out what's out there and, if it is an attack force, we should strike first."

"Most of my men are city dwellers," El Tiburón explained impatiently. "They wouldn't be very effective in the jungle. Some of the refinery workers are from jungle villages, but they aren't fighters. I think my people should stay where they are. The cocaine must be processed. Protecting the fortress is more important than running around in the jungle searching for invaders who have probably already fled. Besides, my people can defend this area against anything short of an assault by a brigade of tanks armed with cannons."

"I do not share your confidence." Pescador frowned. "My soldiers aren't afraid of jungle warfare. The paratroopers are well trained for such warfare and the Sandinistas are all experienced in jungle combat. So are most of the guerrillas."

"The men under your command are subject to your orders, Major," El Tiburón said with a shrug. "If you want to tell your deranged captain to lead a group of men into the jungle to search for invaders, that is your decision. But, I warn you, if they clash with the Savajes, I will not be responsible.''

''I didn't think you would accept responsibility,'' Pescador said, snorting. ''I'll tell the captain to prepare a patrol of my men. *Your* personnel will not be involved, El Tiburón.''

''Very well,'' the *coquito* agreed. ''But tell your men to withdraw if they engage the Indians in battle. Your captain might lose a few men from poison arrows and darts, but if he continues to fight the Savajes, he'll lose more. Besides, I will be very upset if his rash actions cause friction among the Savajes. If this happens, I will hold the captain personally responsible.''

''I think we understand each other,'' the Cuban said dryly.

''I doubt that we shall ever really understand each other,'' El Tiburón said with a chilly smile. ''But that doesn't really matter as long as we both get what we want.''

PHOENIX FORCE AND ALBERTO chopped their way cautiously through the jungle. The Savajes didn't attempt another attack on the commando team. One round had been enough for them.

''This is becoming a bloody bore,'' McCarter complained as he took the point of his knife and hacked at the tangled vines and bushes. ''Are you sure we're heading in the right direction?''

"We're heading south through the Devil's Lair," Alberto answered. "It's the right direction if your information is correct."

"Cordova talked under the influence of scopolamine," Calvin James stated. "Unless he got his directions confused, this is the correct route."

"I'm more worried about the time," Gary Manning admitted. Hours had passed since the men had been able to see the sun overhead, and the shadows were deepening. "It'll be dark soon. I don't really want to stomp around in the jungle at night."

"Doesn't bother me," McCarter commented cheerfully.

"Yeah," Manning muttered. "But you're nuts."

"True," the Briton agreed.

"Darkness will slow us down," Katzenelenbogen acknowledged. "But it could be to our advantage, too. It will help conceal our movement."

"It'll do the same for the enemy," Manning commented. "And we don't have any Starlite scopes or other night-vision gear. If El Tiburón's men have that sort of equipment, we'll be at a definite disadvantage."

"We'd better assume they've got night-vision gear," Encizo said. "After all, the *coquitos* and MERGE can afford to arm their people with the very best."

James sighed. "This is a cheerful conversation. Figure it's too late to head back to the States and tell our boss we pass on this mission?"

"We don't want to do that, mate," McCarter announced as he pushed aside a low-hanging branch. He peered across a valley and smiled at what he saw at the summit of a stone ridge. "Come take a look at this."

The others moved beside McCarter and gazed at the fortress less than two miles away. The elegant stone structure with a swimming pool nearby and grounds dotted with ornate statues could easily have been mistaken for the home of a rich plantation owner. They examined the fortress carefully through the lenses of Tasco binoculars. Guards armed with automatic rifles patrolled the grounds, accompanied by Doberman pinschers with spike-studded collars.

"Notice the sandbags," Katz commented. "They form a circle around the estate. Cover for gunmen if they have to defend the area. Still, I only count four guards on patrol."

"With dogs," Manning added. "That's an additional problem. If those Dobermans get our scent or hear us, they'll alert the sentries. They could smell us *from here* if the wind was blowing in the right direction."

"Yeah," Encizo agreed. "We won't be able to get much closer without the enemy knowing we're here—"

Encizo's words were cut off suddenly as a volley of automatic fire raked their position. One high-velocity slug smashed the binoculars in Manning's hands. Shards scattered across the men as they dropped to the ground. Bullets slashed into the earth and ripped at foliage.

"Not much closer," the Canadian rasped, pulling sharp bits of the shattered plastic from his left palm. Blood dripped from his hand.

"How bad are you hit, man?" James asked as he crawled to Manning. The team medic reached for his first-aid kit.

"Not bad," Manning assured him. "Where the hell did the shots come from?"

"I saw the muzzle-flash about a hundred and fifty yards to the right," Encizo replied. "Only saw one weapon."

"Sniper with a night scope," Manning said as James wrapped a bandage around his damaged hand. "He must have been eager to waste us all, because he had the rifle on full-auto. That was a mistake. Semi is more accurate."

Another barrage of automatic fire cut across their position. The men of Phoenix Force separated, seeking cover among the nearest trees. Manning, James and Encizo rolled in one direction while Katz, McCarter and Alberto moved to another. An explosion erupted about ten yards from their position.

"Grenade," Katz spat through clenched teeth as clods of dirt pelted his back. "They're not within range."

"That means they're probably trying to hold us down so they can get closer," McCarter whispered. He smiled as he held the FMK-3 to his chest. "I like to work close."

"Glad somebody likes this," Alberto said, unable to keep his teeth from chattering.

Another salvo of rapid-fire bullets hammered the area. Slugs struck the trunk of the tree James used for cover. He ducked low and peeked around the edge. The black warrior saw the muzzle-flash of an opponent's weapon.

"So let's play hardball," he growled, pointing his Argentine grenade launcher at the enemy's position. "My serve."

He triggered the weapon. A 40 mm explosive shell streaked through the shadows and crashed close to the position of the muzzle-flash. The grenade exploded. The blast illuminated the hurtling bodies of two men in jungle camouflage uniforms.

Another gunman opened fire from a position two hundred yards left of the first attack team. Encizo immediately fired another grenade at the muzzle-flash. The second explosion ripped apart at least three opponents. Flames crackled along the bark of a tree near the dismembered torso of an enemy.

"*¡Asalta!*" a voice cried from the shadows.

Several figures charged straight for Phoenix Force, shouting a wild battle cry and wielding their weapons as if brandishing banners. Although they were dressed in uniforms and armed with Kalashnikov rifles, they didn't attack like professionals. They seemed unconcerned that they were racing headlong into the guns of their enemy.

"Cannon fodder," Katz muttered as he watched the enemy charge toward him and his men.

Only fanatics would plunge into certain death in such a manner. Whoever they were, Katz knew they weren't *coquito* gunmen. Gangsters were often ruthless, but seldom reckless. He noted they appeared to be Hispanic, and were armed with weapons manufactured by the Communist bloc.

"Terrorists," Katz muttered again. He pointed his FMK-3 at the attackers and called out to his team. "I'll handle this bunch. The rest of you watch for the *real* attack!"

The Israeli hosed the charging figures with 9 mm slugs. Three men died as they ran, nose-diving into death before they struck the earth. Three fanatics fired their AK-47s as they continued to run. One of them dropped to a kneeling stance and aimed his Kalashnikov at Katz. The other two had enough sense to dive for cover behind a boulder.

Katz fired a three-round burst at the kneeling man. Parabellums shredded the man's face and blew his skull to bits. Enemy projectiles still sliced into the jungle behind Katzenelenbogen. The Phoenix Force commander barely noticed. He had been close to death too many times in the past to be unnerved by being shot at. Later, he would feel the cold fingers of fear along his spine and taste the copper and salt in his mouth.

At the moment, he was too busy reacting to the threat to think about his mortality. The two opponents had emerged from the shelter of the rock. Katz emptied the last few rounds of the FMK-3 magazine at them as they advanced. Their bodies jerked and spun from the impact of high-velocity slugs. Then they crumpled lifeless to the ground.

Another wave of attackers scrambled forward, trying to make the most of the natural cover of the surrounding trees and bushes. They moved well, but they were counting on the terrorist charge to distract Phoenix Force. They risked exposing themselves as they dashed from cover to cover, though they didn't present a clear target for more than a split second. Thanks to Katz's instructions to leave the terrorist charge to him, a split second was all Phoenix Force needed to strike.

Manning fired his FAL and drilled three 7.62 mm slugs through the chest of a Sandinista, whose wish that he had never left Nicaragua proved to be his final thought. One of his comrades tried to return fire, but Calvin James already had him in the sights of his M-16.

A trio of 5.56 mm rounds smashed the Sandinista's chin, punctured the hollow of his jawbone and tore into his throat. The Nicaraguan triggerman dropped his weapon and fell backward, both hands clutching his bullet-torn neck. He thrashed about hopelessly as he rapidly drowned in his own blood.

Three Cuban paratroopers moved toward Katz. Alberto saw them approach. He triggered his shotgun too soon, and buckshot struck the ground in front of the trio. The closest man gasped in pain as stray pellets tore into his legs.

The other two Cuban troopers fired their Kalashnikovs at Alberto. The Colombian guide cried out as hot projectiles burned into his stomach and groin. His shotgun tumbled from his fingers as he staggered into a tree trunk, doubled up in agony.

Katz turned to see Alberto slump to the ground. He swung his FMK-3 toward the three enemy soldiers as one of them threw a Soviet F-1 hand grenade at the Israeli's position. The blaster hurtled toward Katz. Alberto leaped into the air to meet it.

It was an incredible feat for a man so badly wounded. The effort racked his bullet-ravaged body with monstrous pain. He failed to catch the grenade, but the F-1 struck his chest and bounced back toward the man who had thrown it.

The grenade landed near the three Cubans. Alberto fell forward and tumbled toward the trio as they desperately grabbed for the fallen grenade. The F-1 exploded before they could touch it. The blast cut one man in half, his entrails spewing from the grisly remains. Another Cuban's head was torn from his shoulders. The third staggered away from the blast, his left hand clamped over his shrapnel-punctured eyes. His right arm had been ripped off at the shoulder. The man uttered a terrible sound, half scream and half whimper, then collapsed. Sprawled on his face in a heap, but not dismembered, was the dead body of the courageous Alberto.

Four enemy soldiers—two Sandinistas, a Cuban corporal and a terrorist who had formerly served with the widespread fanatic group that called itself Condor—attempted to circle around the Phoenix Force position to ambush the commandos from behind. They moved in a wide arc, slipping behind a cluster of giant ferns and creeping past a column of walnut trees.

David McCarter waited behind the trunk of the thickest tree. He held his breath as the enemy passed the tree. The Briton clenched the pistol grip of the Wildcat crossbow in his right fist and the Browning automatic in his left. He stepped from behind the tree, aimed the crossbow and fired.

The Condor veteran at the tail end of the group suddenly dropped his AK-47 and stiffened as if snapping to attention. The others turned and saw their comrade fall forward. The short shaft of a crossbow bolt jutted from the base of his skull. The steel tip of the projectile was buried deep in his brain.

McCarter extended his left arm, snap-aimed and fired the Browning. A former member of the British Olympic pistol team, McCarter possessed extraordinary marksmanship with a handgun. He pumped two 9 mm slugs into the chest of one Sandinista and drilled another round into the belly of the corporal from Havana. At the same time, his right hand grabbed the pistol grip of the FMK-3 that hung from a shoulder strap.

The wounded Cuban raised his PPSh-41 submachine gun while the surviving Sandinista swung an American-made M-16 toward McCarter. The Briton fired his Argentine chattergun before either man could trigger his weapon. Parabellums punched through flesh and pulverized organs. The pair fell, their bodies draping the corpses of their fallen comrades.

Rafael Encizo opened fire on three opponents, including a muscular man wearing three gray stars on the shoulder of his uniform. It was the insignia of a captain in the Cuban army. The officer jumped to cover behind a boulder. One of his men followed his example, but the other trooper caught two parabellums in the center of his chest.

Mortally wounded, the soldier fell, dying while his comrades returned fire. Encizo had already moved to a new position. The Phoenix pro ducked behind a tree trunk and crept along a row of cinchona bushes. He saw an enemy trooper rise from the boulder to fire his AK-47 at the position Encizo had formerly occupied.

Encizo triggered his FMK-3. A trio of 9 mm rounds slammed into the Cuban gunman. One bullet performed a high-velocity lobotomy and punched an exit wound at the crown of the guy's head. The soldier dropped his AK-47 and fell beside the boulder, brains pouring from his shattered skull.

"¡Eh, capitán!" Encizo shouted in Spanish. "You're all alone now. Throw out your gun and surrender."

The Cuban officer responded by firing his Makarov pistol in the direction of Encizo's voice. The Phoenix fighter dashed to the cover of the tree and blasted a quick burst of FMK-3 rounds at the boulder. Encizo didn't want to kill the captain. The man was more valuable alive. But the Phoenix warrior didn't intend to sacrifice his own life to try to capture a prisoner because the guy *might* possess useful information.

Bullets ricocheted off stone. The Cuban officer yelled with pain and anger when chips of rock pelted his hand. His fist opened, and the Makarov fell from his grasp. Encizo quickly rushed forward, subgun pointed at the captain's position.

"¡Alto!" he warned. "Step forward . . . slowly."

"You speak Spanish like a Cuban," the captain remarked as he moved from behind the boulder, rubbing his injured hand.

"I've had years of practice," Encizo replied. He strained his eyes, trying to see the officer better in the dim light. The man seemed familiar. . . .

"Traitor," the captain hissed and spat at Encizo's feet.

A streak of moonlight fell across the officer's face, displaying his swarthy, handsome features and the strawberry-colored, heart-shaped birthmark on his cheek. Encizo stared at him, astonished. He recognized the captain.

"Raúl?" Encizo asked, stepping closer to allow the light to fall on his face as well. "Do you remember me, Raúl?"

"You know my name?" The captain frowned. "But I do not know you...."

"It was a long time ago, Raúl," Encizo began, his voice almost pleading with his captive. "A very long time—"

The captain lashed a fast roundhouse kick at the FMK-3 and knocked the weapon from Encizo's grasp. He slashed a cross-body karate chop to the side of Encizo's skull. The Phoenix fighter staggered back from the blow, and his opponent thrust stiffened fingers at Encizo's throat.

The veteran warrior dodged the deadly spear-hand thrust and swiftly grabbed Raúl's wrist. He turned sharply and adroitly hurled the captain over his hip. Raúl hit the ground hard. Encizo quickly twisted his opponent's arm in a jujitsu wrist lock.

"Raúl, please..." Encizo urged.

The officer ignored him and twisted his body around. Encizo held on while the other man struggled. Bone popped at the joint of Raúl's wrist. Encizo grimaced, as if he suffered more pain than his opponent.

Raúl lashed out a boot, and it crashed into the side of Encizo's face. The kick knocked Encizo off his feet. He landed on his back, his head throbbing with pain.

Raúl rose, his dislocated wrist cradled in his other hand. He glared at Encizo and prepared to throw another kick at the dazed Phoenix warrior.

"Freeze, you bastard!" Calvin James shouted as he aimed his M-16 at the captain.

The officer slowly raised his arms and impassively watched James approach. Encizo struggled to his feet. Raúl noticed James's eyes turn toward his fellow Phoenix Force pro. Seizing the opportunity, the captain dived headlong into a cluster of ferns and rolled down a shallow gorge.

"Son of a bitch!" James spat as he aimed his rifle at the fleeing officer.

"No!" Encizo cried. He grabbed the rifle barrel and pointed the gun toward the sky. "Don't shoot him!"

"Hey, man!" the black warrior snapped as he shook the gun free of his partner's grasp. "You crackin' up or something?"

"Don't shoot him, Calvin," Encizo urged. "He's my brother."

17

"Your brother?" Gary Manning said with surprise.

Phoenix Force had completed mopping up the enemy, and Rafael Encizo and Calvin James were explaining the situation concerning the fierce Cuban captain.

"My younger brother Raúl," Encizo confirmed. "He's ten years younger than me, about two inches taller and he kicks like a mule."

"Put some of this on your cheek," James said, handing Encizo a tube of ointment. "Don't think you've got any bones or teeth broken, but your face is gonna be sore for a while."

"Are you certain this paratrooper captain is your brother?" Yakov Katzenelenbogen inquired as he inspected one of the discarded AK-47 rifles. "Last time you saw him he was only a boy."

"Absolutely," Encizo replied. "Raúl resembled our father, even as a child, and he had a heart-shaped birthmark on his cheek. I'm certain the man I saw is my brother, Raúl Encizo."

"You've never talked much about your family, Rafael," Manning remarked. "I don't recall you ever mentioned Raúl before."

"When Castro took control of Cuba," Encizo replied, "most of my family were killed. I joined the freedom fighters in the hills. My two younger sisters and my brother, the youngest in the family, were taken to a 'reeducation center.' Apparently Raúl has been fully indoctrinated with communism."

"I'm sorry, Rafael," Katz told him. "It must be quite a shock to find out your brother is on the other side."

"At least I know he's still alive," Encizo said with a thin smile.

David McCarter had been the first of Encizo and James's mates to approach them after Encizo's discovery of his brother's identity. After Manning and Katz had arrived on the scene, McCarter had gone for an inspection of the arena of the recent fight. Now he returned to the others, carrying two AK-47 rifles as well as his own weapons. He placed the confiscated guns on the ground.

"Alberto is dead," he announced.

"I know," Katz said with a shake of his head. "He fought like a lion and took three of the enemy with him. He saved my life back there."

"Well, I hate to point this out," McCarter continued, turning toward the mansion, "but this mission isn't over yet."

"Right," Katz confirmed. "Let's get back to work."

"What about my brother?" Encizo asked.

"We'll take him alive if we can," Katz answered.

"Raúl was only a child when the Communists took him," Encizo insisted. "It's not his fault."

"He's dangerous, Rafael," the Israeli insisted. "He almost killed you, didn't he?"

"I was taken off guard..." Encizo began lamely, aware that his excuse didn't make the situation any better.

"Like I said," Katz repeated, "we'll take him alive if we can."

"I gathered up some of the enemy rifles and found some Soviet-made F-1 grenades on some of those blokes," McCarter stated. "Figured we might need them when we hit the fortress."

"Yeah," James muttered. "The element of surprise is sure blown to hell now."

THE GUN BATTLE two miles from the fortress had caused a flurry of activity at El Tiburón's estate and at the cocaine refinery near the *coquito*'s lair. The Shark's gunmen rushed around the grounds, checking defenses. Some set up mounted machine guns among the sandbags. El Tiburón issued orders to his pilots to make certain the helicopters were ready to fly in the unlikely event that escape would be necessary.

At the refinery, near-chaos set in. Despite the pleas of Napoli, the chemist, and the threats of El Tiburón's enforcers, the peasant workers were panic-stricken and desperate to escape. They hadn't been hired to fight. They were former rubber workers, emerald miners and coffee pickers, not gunmen.

The laborers bolted in all directions. Napoli ordered them to return to their stations and tried to stop the thugs posted at the refinery from firing their weapons. Neither group listened to the chemist. Gunmen opened fire at fleeing workers. A stream of automatic bullets cut down two peasants as they fled from the lab. The slugs also pierced the wall and struck a bottle of ether inside the lab.

Sparks ignited the volatile substance, and the lab exploded in a terrible fireball that consumed Napoli and half a dozen laborers and gunmen. Hydrochloric acid, gasoline, kerosene and ammonia were also ignited by the blast. The entire refinery went up in flames. Burning debris showered to earth after the explosions. Human torches staggered from the area, flames dancing across their flesh and hair.

"Jesus!" Calvin James gasped as they spotted the orange glow of the conflagration in the distance. "What happened?"

"Somebody just provided us with a distraction," Katzenelenbogen replied. "Let's take advantage of it."

Phoenix Force approached the fortress from the west, aware that most of El Tiburón's people would be looking east toward the burning refinery. The guard dogs were virtually useless, panicked by the explosions and the stench of burning chemicals. The animals barked and pulled at their leashes, creating more confusion within the compound.

"*¡No dispara!*" Encizo shouted to the gunmen stationed by the sandbags at the west wing of the fortress. "Don't shoot! Captain Encizo abandoned us out here. We're coming in!"

"Come in!" a thug replied. "Hurry!"

The camouflage uniforms of the men of Phoenix Force were similar to those worn by the Cuban and Sandinista troops led by Captain Encizo. The Colombian hoodlums at the wall didn't realize they had given permission for five invaders to enter the compound. They didn't suspect anything was wrong until the men were actually climbing over the sandbags.

"*¡Cristo!*" exclaimed a thug stationed behind an M-60 machine gun. He reached for the trigger mechanism.

A crossbow bolt struck the guy in the side of the neck. He tumbled into one of his comrades, blood spurting from a severed carotid artery. Another hoodlum raised his Mendoza submachine gun as Rafael Encizo hurled a machete. The steel point pierced the thug's chest, and the heavy blade sunk deep into flesh, wreaking massive tissue damage. The Mendoza fell unfired, and its owner collapsed against the sandbags.

The third goon pushed aside the body of the crossbow victim and reached for a holstered Star PD on his hip. Gary Manning swiftly closed in and swung the walnut stock of his FAL rifle. The butt stroke caught the guy across the bridge of the nose. Blood spurted from his nostrils, and he fell dead at Manning's feet.

James shifted the M-60 around to point it at the parade field, then stationed himself behind the weapon and waved the others on. He placed his M-16 by his right knee and lined up his grenades next to the rifle. He checked the ammunition belt to the M-60 to be certain there were no knots. After that there was nothing to do but wait.

The other four men of Phoenix Force walked across the compound without attracting a second glance. The enemy assumed that the refinery had been destroyed by the assault force that had fought the Savaje Indians and the patrol led by Captain Encizo. They were sure the strike force would approach from the east.

Hoodlums at the machine gun nest by the east wall opened fire with their M-60. Tracer rounds sliced through the night sky as the thugs blasted away at the shapes that ran from the fiery remnants of the refinery. The overzealous triggerman didn't realize they were gunning down harmless workers who had survived the explosion.

The men stationed at the third machine gun nest, by a wall of sandbags to the north, were watching their comrades to the east slaughter victims outside the fortress. Other thugs tried to control the nearly hysterical guard dogs or simply waited in reserve in case they were needed.

Manning strolled toward the front door of the mansion. Two soldiers stationed by the entrance eyed the Canadian dubiously. Knowing how little he resembled a typical Colombian, Manning decided not to get any closer to the guards. He leaned against a marble statue of a naked woman and pretended to watch the machine gunners at the east wall.

McCarter and Katz strode toward the north wall while Encizo headed for the east, his Argentine grenade launcher casually dangling from his right fist. McCarter had discarded his Wildcat crossbow and carried his FMK-3 subgun.

"Ready for some fireworks?" Katz whispered to the Briton as he took an M-59 fragmentation grenade from his belt.

"This party needs some excitement," McCarter replied.

"That can be arranged," the Israeli said, pulling the pin from his grenade.

He popped the spoon and held the M-59 for two seconds before he hurled it at the machine gun nest at the north wall. He and McCarter dashed to cover behind a jeep. The grenade exploded, blasting apart the thugs at the machine gun nest. Twisted metal and mutilated corpses scattered across the sandbags.

The explosion was the signal Encizo and Manning were waiting for. The Cuban warrior raised his grenade launcher and fired a 40 mm shell into the machine gun nest at the east wall. The blast sent sandbags, bodies and mangled weaponry hurtling from the wall.

Manning promptly swung his FAL rifle at the sentries by the door and opened fire. The Canadian marksman nailed each man with three 7.62 mm slugs through the chest. Their bodies slumped to the marble porch as Manning rushed to the door.

Working rapidly, the Canadian demolitions expert placed C-4 plastic explosive at the door hinges. He inserted a pencil detonator with a special blasting cap and set the timing dial for ten seconds, then he dashed back to the cover of the statue.

Manning literally ran into one of El Tiburón's goons, who had also ducked behind the stone figure for shelter. Both men grunted with surprise when they collided. Manning quickly rammed a fist into his opponent's solar plexus and slammed the guy's head into the marble lady's breast. The thug's eyes rolled up in their sockets, and he slumped unconscious.

The door opened, and three hoods armed with subguns emerged. The C-4 exploded before they could step from the porch. The blast ripped away the door and transformed the Colombian syndicate flunkies into flying chunks of gory meat.

Half a dozen thugs, two of them accompanied by guard dogs, hurried toward this most recent explosion. By then Katz and McCarter were on their way to join Manning. The Briton fired into the group with his FMK-3. Men screamed, and a Doberman whimpered as 9 mm slugs smashed through flesh. Three gunmen were killed outright. Another doubled up in agony, his guts spilling from two slugs in his lower abdomen. The other two managed to drop to the ground without catching any parabellums.

The Doberman lunged at McCarter's throat. He raised his FMK-3 to block the animal's assault. The beast crashed into the subgun, knocking it from McCarter's hands.

The Doberman hit the ground, turned sharply and leaped again. Swiftly McCarter pulled his machete from its sheath and delivered a fast cross-body stroke. The blade hacked through flesh and bone. The dog's head struck the ground and rolled for two feet. Its body twitched briefly, blood oozing from the stump of its neck.

The two surviving gunmen were almost on their feet, their weapons pointed at McCarter. Before they could open fire, the metallic chatter of an automatic weapon erupted. The pair collapsed, their chests and faces torn open by 9 mm slugs. Katz triggered his FMK-3 to make certain they would never get up again.

"Thanks, mate," McCarter called to Katz as he retrieved his FMK-3.

"My pleasure," the Israeli assured him. "Shall we check out the inside of the Shark's home?"

"It's what I live for," McCarter assured him.

The pair moved toward Manning as he lobbed a concussion grenade through the doorway. The blast guaranteed that no one would be lurking just inside the door, waiting to attack them. Manning, McCarter and Katz jogged to the doorway.

A group of El Tiburón's goons several yards away spotted the three Phoenix Force commandos just as they entered the building. The Colombian triggermen charged in pursuit of the trio. They didn't notice Calvin James until the black warrior opened fire with the M-60 machine gun.

Vicious salvos of 7.62 mm rounds crashed into the hoodlums. Their bodies convulsed like puppets in the hands of a lunatic. James shifted the M-60 to fire into another group of opponents headed toward his position. Four Colombian killers crumbled to the ground. Three others dived behind a marble table near the swimming pool.

James quickly yanked the pin from a grenade and hurled it at the enemy's position. He braced himself behind the M-60 and waited for the grenade to blow. It exploded near the marble table. The blast pitched the goons into the open. Two lay dead or dying. The third staggered to his feet and limped toward the pool.

Calvin James triggered the machine gun. Half a dozen high-velocity slugs ripped across the Colombian's back, splitting his spine in four sections. The impact spun the guy around and hurled him into the pool. His body floated on the water as a cloud of crimson formed around it.

Just then, from the rear of the mansion, came the unmistakable roar of a helicopter taking off. Blades whirling, a Bell UH-1 chopper rose above the estate, then climbed higher into the night sky, flying south toward Peru. Rafael Encizo raised his FMK-3 at the aircraft but held his fire. The chopper was already out of range.

What was it Juan Cordova had told them about the helipad at El Tiburón's estate? Encizo asked himself. Then he remembered: it was large enough to accommodate two copters. Encizo headed for the rear of the building, where he could already hear the rushing thunder of rotor blades.

He peered cautiously around the corner of the big house. Another Bell copter waited on a paved landing pad. Two men emerged from the rear door of the building. One was stocky with a pug face and an Uzi submachine gun in his fists. The other was older but looked as fit as an athlete, and he carried himself with the dignity of a man accustomed to being in charge. One hand held a leather briefcase, the other held a derringer.

"Who the hell left in the other helicopter?" El Tiburón demanded as he and the bodyguard strode swiftly across the pad.

"Major Pescador and the paratrooper, Captain Encizo, just took off, *jefe*," the bodyguard explained. "One of them must be a pilot, because we found Gomez lying in the workshop. His neck had been broken."

"Treacherous Cuban bastards," El Tiburón growled. "We never should have trusted the Communists—"

"Drop your guns!" Encizo shouted. *"¡Ahora!"*

El Tiburón's bodyguard whirled and swung his Uzi toward Encizo's voice. The Cuban warrior triggered his Argentine subgun. Three 9 mm rounds punched a row of bullet holes in the thug's chest. El Tiburón dropped his derringer and briefcase and raised his hands. He was well aware that attempting to outshoot an opponent armed with a submachine gun was folly.

"You must be El Tiburón," Encizo remarked as he approached the gangster, his FMK-3 pointed at the Shark's belly. "I heard your stooge call you *jefe*. You're one big fish that isn't getting away."

"So I am under arrest?" El Tiburón asked, holding his hands at shoulder level. "I think you're making a mistake, *señor*. I do not own this place. I am not even a citizen of Colombia. See for yourself. My passport is in my jacket pocket. I am a Bolivian—"

"You are a *coquito* piece of shit," Encizo told him, "and I'll happily send you to hell if you give me half a reason. Lie on your belly and spread your arms and legs."

El Tiburón frowned at the affront to his dignity as he started to kneel.

From the corner of his eye Encizo caught movement, and he turned his head toward the helicopter. For an instant he wondered if he had simply been distracted by the whirling rotor blades. Then he saw the figure at the sliding door of the chopper carriage. A helmet and visor covered the man's head. The chopper pilot held a pistol, aimed at Encizo.

The Phoenix force commando whirled and fired a rapid volley of full-auto slugs into the pilot. The man's body was thrown back against the carriage of the helicopter, then slid to the ground.

Still more standing than kneeling, El Tiburón took advantage of the distraction. He lunged forward and seized Encizo's FMK-3. The gangster pushed the weapon toward the sky and aimed a knee at Encizo's groin. The Cuban shifted his thigh to protect his genitals and shoved at the weapon, trying to slam it across El Tiburón's face.

The Bolivian turned slightly as he rode out the motion, wrenching Encizo's wrists. The weapon slipped from the fingers of the Phoenix pro. He slammed a knee kick into El Tiburón's tailbone. The blow jarred the *coquito* and weakened his balance. Encizo pulled hard, spun his opponent around and swung a left hook at El Tiburón's face.

Knuckles cracked against the Bolivian hood's jawbone, but he responded with a snap kick to Encizo's rib cage. The Phoenix fighter gasped and staggered backward. El Tiburón reached inside his jacket and swiftly drew his fighting dagger.

Encizo unsnapped the restraining strap of his K-Bar knife. His draw was awkward because he wasn't accustomed to the knife or its sheath. El Tiburón slashed at Encizo's face. The Cuban weaved away from the blade, and El Tiburón quickly lunged for his stomach.

Steel clashed on steel as Encizo blocked the dagger thrust with his blade. He stepped forward to the right and deftly slashed the Bowie across El Tiburón's chest. The Bolivian was also moving, dodging Encizo's blade. He took a swipe at the Cuban's neck.

Encizo raised a forearm. Pain stung as the sharp steel sliced flesh. Encizo danced backward, not sparing a glance at his wounded arm. The warm wetness told him the cut was bleeding. Blood also laced El Tiburón's chest, but the Bolivian smiled.

"Do you like the Shark's Tooth?" El Tiburón asked. "It thirsts for your blood. Come and feed it."

Encizo didn't respond. He executed a short stab at El Tiburón's face to distract him and followed it with a swift slash at the other man's wrist. El Tiburón ducked his arm beneath the flashing steel and lunged at Encizo's belly. Encizo dodged, and the blade bit into flesh under his ribs without penetrating deeply.

The Cuban ignored the pain and delivered a slash to the triceps muscle of El Tiburón's upper arm. The Bolivian gasped in pain and retreated. Both opponents bled from their several wounds. El Tiburón nodded with mute respect for Encizo's skill.

The gangster crouched low and thrust at Encizo's ribs. The Phoenix pro slashed to counter the attack, although he suspected it was a feint. In a flash, El Tiburón tossed the knife to his other hand and lunged from the left. Encizo swung his Bowie swiftly and blocked the attack with the flat of his blade.

The Cuban followed with a solid left hook to his opponent's face. El Tiburón staggered. Encizo snap-kicked him between the legs. A rasping moan escaped from the Bolivian's throat, but he still stabbed at Encizo's stomach. The Phoenix Force vet weaved away from the blade. Suddenly he clamped his arm across El Tiburón's wrist.

Encizo scooped up El Tiburón's forearm in the crook of his elbow and trapped the Bolivian's wrist with his arm. The gangster's left fist and the dagger were pinned under the Cuban's armpit. Desperately his right hand clawed at Encizo's eyes, but the Cuban blocked with his left forearm and grabbed the back of El Tiburón's neck.

He pulled the Bolivian forward and snaked his arm across the cocaine merchant's back. Encizo embraced him as if trying to comfort a friend. El Tiburón shuddered, his face pressed against Encizo's right shoulder. The dagger fell from the *coquito*'s hand, and his body went limp in Encizo's arms. The Cuban pushed him away.

El Tiburón fell to the pavement. Encizo's knife was lodged in his chest with five inches of steel buried in his heart. The Cuban stepped back, breathing hard. His shirt and trousers were soaked with crimson. Some of the blood was his own, but most had poured over him from the deep wound inflicted upon his opponent.

"Rafael!" Katz cried as he and McCarter ran from the rear door of the building. "My God, what happened?"

"I'm okay," Encizo replied, attempting a weak smile. "It's not as bad as it looks. Is everybody else all right?"

"All of our blokes are," McCarter confirmed. "Most of the enemy are dead, but we've got a few prisoners for General Torres to question. Unfortunately, it looks like El Tiburón got away in that bloody helicopter."

"No, he didn't," Encizo said, pointing at the dead *coquito*. "Nobody got away except two Cuban officers. One of them was my brother."

Encizo's voice was unsteady. It wasn't just the aftermath of his duel with El Tiburón. It wasn't the crushing fatigue that hit as the adrenaline level dropped, the relief that he was still alive, the satisfaction that the nightmare merchant of death lay dead at his feet. Something inside him mourned. *Raúl,* he thought. *My brother* . . . After all these years, he had found Raúl, as his enemy.

Katz rested his left hand on Encizo's shoulder, just for a few seconds. Then he unclipped the two-way radio from his belt. "Mission accomplished, gentlemen," he declared. "Let's ask the general to send his flying taxi so we can go home."

4 FREE BOOKS
1 FREE GIFT
NO RISK
NO OBLIGATION
NO KIDDING